Hotel Curtains

Pat Jourdan

patjourdan.wordpress.com

Acknowledgements

With thanks to the editors of the magazines where these stories first appeared: The Weary Blues, Café Lit, Pachinko and The Best of Café Lit 8.

'Grounded' won second place in the Michael McLaverty Short Story Award.

The cover photograph is reproduced by kind permission of Rene Asmussen, asmussenfotografi@gmail.com

Hotel Curtains

Pat Jourdan

Short Stories

Also by Pat Jourdan

Novels

Finding Out

A Small Inheritance

Maryland Street

Poetry

The Bedsit Girl

The Bedsit

Ainnir Anthology

Turpentine

The Cast-Iron Shore

Liverpool Poets 2008

Citizeness

Short Stories

Average Sunday Afternoon

Taking the Field

Rainy Pavements

The Fog Index

for
Amelia Hull-Hewitt, Hunter Jourdan & Inigo Jourdan

Contents

Airport Sandwiches

Margo turned up early at her father's house at the edge of Johannesburg without much luggage. Stan was surprised how much she had changed after her divorce, but then it was quite a while ago. They sat outside on the veranda in the evenings planning his visit to his brother in Montreal, a last chance to meet as they were both in their late seventies. Margo had persuaded him and even suggested going with him as encouragement.

"It'll be a wonderful thing to do, meeting after twenty years! You'll both be so glad and you'll wonder why it took so long – Uncle Oscar will be really pleased you made the effort!" Margo cheered him up. She set to work on her laptop, finding out flight times, connections, printing out tickets and boarding passes, comparing currency dealers, travel insurance, looking for somewhere to stay overnight in Montreal and, of course, ordering new suitcases for him. "At least you've got a ten-year passport already, or we'd be stuck here waiting," she added. "It's a good job you went to that conference in Canberra after you retired. We'll need visas for Canada too." Stan was impressed how business-like his daughter was, how capable. She even organised new clothes for him, taking him into town with her and going into department stores gents' outfitting, seeing that he bought outfits that would impress his brother. "I'll just dash off to the travel agents

9

now about the visas while you try on something warm for Canada wear." Margo was like a whirlwind.

They managed to get through Johannesburg airport with the least amount of trouble, he was surprised.

"We're on our way at last!" Stan said, a bit relieved it was really happening. Now, in Stansted airport Stan sat watching the people opposite, sitting in the brightly lit café that served real meals. He could see families sitting down to large plates with hot dinners, set next to desserts and drinks. Drifts of assorted food aromas reached him. Perhaps later he could go across and manage to have something to eat, but he had to ration out his money to last until tomorrow. All the other outlets were coffee bars, sandwich shops, newsagents, money-changers and boutiques selling all kinds of luxury goods. The never-ending stream of passengers entertained him; or at least they had at first. Now it was getting later, five in the afternoon here, something like eight o'clock in the morning in his jet-lagged bloodstream.

He still could not work out how Margo had happened to go off with his passport and all his tickets. She also had most of his money as he had packed his jacket and only had a little space in his waistcoat pockets.

"I'll take care of all that, Dad," Margo had said. "I've got this handbag, after all it's more convenient if I carry the lot together. And you shouldn't be carrying so much loose cash, you might lose it." She kept mentioning how forgetful he was these days, and she was right. Ever since she had come to stay she was pointing out how often he could not remember where he put things and how his memory was really befuddled. Often he was puzzled at this; living alone, he had not noticed it until Margo had come to stay. Suddenly he was losing keys, forgetting to lock doors, mistaking the right time, it was a catalogue of mishaps. As she pointed out, all the more reason to go and visit his only brother while he could still manage the journey.

It had taken some courage to go and contact the enquiry desk and ask about the two o'clock flight to Montreal. But the check-in clerk could not help.

"That's gone several minutes ago. It's up on the board, you can see it on the Departures section," the assistant pointed out. "If you did not turn up on time there would have been a public announcement. Didn't you hear it?" Stan was sure he had not heard his own name called but these days he was becoming more doubtful day by day.

"I've been here in the departures hall all the time, heard nothing at all. You say the flight has gone? My daughter's on it, she has my passport and the tickets too."

He did not mention the money, the precious rands changed into Canadian dollars. "Her mobile won't be working while she's on the flight, I suppose, so it's useless trying to get into contact until they land." The enquiry assistant looked at him carefully and being both kindly and efficient, made a call to Montreal arrivals hall that Ms Margo Naidoo, flying from Johannesburg via Stansted, should be contacted as soon as possible to come to their passenger counter and produce her father's passport and tickets to the authorities in Canada.

"Well, that's all we can do so far, you'll be able to do something about that tomorrow morning. I'm sorry, that's as much as we can do at present. You see, right now you have no confirmed travel identity and you cannot buy another ticket without your passport or credit card. We have to wait until we have confirmation." She looked over the passenger details of the flight again, but could find no entry for any Stan Govender.

"Are you sure this was the right flight? There is another one later this evening. It has to have a changeover in Reykjavic 19.30 and arrives at Pierre Trudeau International the next day – you'll have quite a wait, unfortunately" But that flight was also without any trace of his name. While Stan waited for any news he had time to think and wonder. How had Margo been separated from him in the luggage hall?

He had been waiting for her at the carousel for their suitcases and she had been lost in the crowd. He wheeled the overladen trolley into the airport hall, thinking Margo had probably gone off to the toilets but she had not reappeared. Stan loitered at the arrivals concourse along with all the taxi drivers and tour representatives. Nearly an hour had gone by before he accepted that something had gone seriously wrong. He did not have enough money to go off to a nearby hotel now, either – Stansted had several in the grounds. Margo had taken his wallet, for security, she said.

"I'll keep all the important things together, Dad, so you don't lose anything." He sat with the trolley piled up with Margo's and his own suitcases, sure that the mess would all be settled in the morning.

Getting into conversation with a middle-aged woman at the next table as they sat outside a café, Stan told her he was stranded here because his daughter had gone off to Montreal with his ticket and passport. He was stuck overnight with nowhere to stay.

"I'm just going to sit here, have to sleep in a chair, she'll be getting in touch as soon as they land and the mix-up can be settled. Just got to last the night here," he smiled. The woman was worried, though, and went across to a security attendant nearby, telling him of the old man's plight.

"He's not a youngster and he can't be left alone in an airport all night sitting in a plastic seat. In fact he doesn't look at all healthy to me. I'd help, but my own flight to Vienna is due soon and I've got to be off."

"I'll have a word with him. You mean that old guy over there by Pret-á-manger with the gigantic luggage trolley? We have little overnight cabins for situations like this, anyone ill or overnight staff having to stay. Don't worry, we'll look after him." She went off to the take-away café and came back with teas and large sandwiches of cheese and tomato in wholemeal bread.

"It's the healthiest version I could find. I don't know if you take sugar, there's two sachets here," she said as she sat down next to him again. "I love these airport sandwiches. I wonder where they get this bread from, is it something special? It tastes so different from any at home." Stan accepted the tribute of food gratefully. He had not realised how out-of-pocket he was. A few rand still in his pocket; not enough for a meal in any currency. It occurred to him that in this quickly-moving crowd he could sit here unnoticed as the world walked past. No one would see him. The attendant showed Stan into a cabin, explaining he would be called for at first light. He would be safe in the forest of cabins until the morning.

"Yes, this one is called 'Larch.' They're all called after trees, Birch, Oak, Ash, Fir, Holly, Rowan, Willow and so on - they're all here." He helped Stan wheel the luggage into the little cabin and left Stan sitting on the bed, stranded in this indoor forest. He was worn out and beginning to be far more worried now than he had been earlier. Bits of questions were falling into a strange jigsaw.

Opening one of Margo's three large cases, he found it full of old books; another was full of shoes. In her other case there were no clothes, no toiletries, just newspapers and magazines. It was the luggage of a woman who was going to disappear.

.

Winning the Lottery

Uncle Lionel was not enthusiastic about Adam coming to work in his garage.

"For one person in this family, you're going to have to do something else." Things were difficult now that Bernard, his father had been killed in a boating accident. "You're only going to meet local guys whose cars and lorries are up the spout." He advised Adam to go and work in the new hotel. "I'll put in a good word. You can get a respectable, easy indoors job there as a waiter and you'll keep your hands clean too."

Adam could see no sense in this.

"But what's that going to lead to, except for some free food? It's not a real man's job, is it?" He wanted to join the other lads in Uncle Lionel's garage. It was the centre of gossip on the island and he did not want to be away from some of the men who he had known since childhood. But Adam did as he was advised and at least his mother was pleased. His sister, Clarisse, was quiet about the change of plan. She helped with their mother's dressmaking at home.

The job turned out to be not so bad though the hours were long. All day he was at the mercy of international travellers who demanded perfect service. Adam soon acquired an all-weather, all-day and night smile as he attended to their needs and wants. Waiting at table for every meal, delivering drinks and snacks to individual rooms, serving at banquets and conferences, his days and nights drifted past. His few days off were spent with his family, and he always brought them gifts of fancy food from the kitchens, surplus to requirement and some clothes left by visitors.. Uncle Lionel called round.

"How's it going?"

"Can get hectic at times. But I've got used to feeding off marvellous food and drinks."

"Met any rich women yet?"

"What do you mean?" Adam laughed. Uncle Lionel drew nearer, conspiratorially.

"You know, there's going to be rich white women drifting through, looking for someone. They don't even know who they're looking for. You just make sure it's you she's looking for, that's all." Adam saw what he meant. He had seen how the waitresses flirted with the male guests and had assumed it led to nothing. Emilia, his mother had dropped hints, but Adam had been too naïve to pick up what she meant.

"What's sauce for the goose is sauce for the gander, our Adam," she told him. "Just you keep your eye out. You never know." And so it happened.

Adam saw the two new English ladies at breakfast. He was not allocated to their table but he asked Jules to change over with him. He was charm itself and both women blossomed under his never-ending cheerful attention. Adam was ready at their table for every meal; this morning he was fussing with a fresh bunch of flowers.

"These blue flowers match your eyes" he added, turning to the taller woman. Her friend, Helen giggled.

"It looks to me like you've got yourself a beau already," she said to Marianne.

It was Marianne who had arranged the visit.
Her husband was away yet again, his construction business often taking him abroad. She had got used to his many absences – and his money. No questions asked, all bills paid. She suspected he was having an affair but did not know precisely what to do next. This island getaway holiday was a break from the worries. Helen had been easy to persuade to come along.

"I need to think things over," Marianne said.

Soon Adam and Marianne were spending what little free time he had, together. They often sat at a small bar, along the coast, its terrace set under the trees for shade. He knew these extra-private places, he said, that tourists did not find. Their free time was secret to themselves. Helen knew to be discreet; she was content with her own company and had a thick airport novel to read. Plus, Marianne had arranged to pay their hotel fees.

And that was how it developed. Adam led Marianne to another bar near the shore. A few locals sat outside playing cards. It was painted with a light blue wash which contrasted with the bougainvillea around it.

"It's up for sale, you know," he pointed out. He sensed Marianne was falling in love with him, deeper and deeper by the day. She told Helen now, in a polite way, to get lost.

"I've met the perfect man for my future. I'm going to move here." They planned to get married and run the bar-by-the-sea. All Marianne had to do was to get divorced. The divorce papers were served immediately she got home – Helen was sworn to secrecy about this affair. It took several months to settle, but Marianne managed a couple of visits to the island meanwhile.

"You just sign your name here ...and ...here," the solicitor said in the township nearby. Marianne, in the throes of newly-wedded bliss, signed the wedding licence and right afterwards she signed the purchase of the shoreline bar and all its lock, stock and barrels.

Of course Adam had long had his own woman and three children up in the high hills, a hidden part of his life. He had won the lottery. It had been so easy. Everything was entered in his sole name as the island's constitution said that only local people could purchase such important community property. Marianne was totally confident in him, their joint bank account already set up.

The opulent green and fluorescent blossom, never-ending sunshine, the soft lap of the tide; it was all even more heavenly as Adam was now going to be owning a part of it forever.

He turned up every three weeks or so, always with some new present; even more expensive if he had been away for longer. A trip to Spain meant a soft leather coat; Hong Kong was a diamond ring, patterned into a small pagoda of diamonds, but diamonds nevertheless. Other trips abroad brought a Pari Patek watch, a diamond bracelet and a mink coat.

But all is not perfect in paradise; Louise was cross when he let slip that the mink he had bought for his wife was a blue mink, not the common kind he had given Louise. Perhaps that was the first slight rift. There was of course the usual couple of bottles of whisky and brandy, the very special bottle of perfume.

"Always *Joy,*" she said to Emma in the office of Reads Logistics, "It's the most expensive perfume in the world. He always has to buy the same one for his wife and me so she never picks up a stray scent and becomes suspicious."

Or was it when he told her Sandra was pregnant in spite of Harry earlier having told her that they slept apart, or at least in separate beds? It is as much a shock for a mistress to think her man is fornicating with his own wife as it is a shock for the wife to discover there is a mistress on the scene.

These drawbacks were massing in the background but the real killer of passion was when Louise started having affairs with other men. It happened by accident: she had to go out occasionally to pubs or parties. Easter Monday, Whit weekend, August Bank Holiday and of course all the days from Christmas to New Year she was supposed to stay alone while Harry and Sandra played at house. It was this break in the thread of fidelity that made all the difference. Looking round the walls of the flat became like looking at prison walls.

Louise looked forward to Harry's visits less and less. It became predictable – dinner at a restaurant she had to book for him, as his name had to be kept secret – and then back to his permanently reserved hotel suite or her own flat. Her own flat; but bought and donated by him. His only rule was that she should have a job to keep her occupied and mask her real status.

"I don't want you sitting round just waiting for me to turn up," Harry said, "You've got to have something to occupy you." She obediently got a job in an transport logistics agents typing out inventories and advertisements. But now it had grown worse. She told her closest friend, the only woman in the office,

"I have to get a bit drunk before we go up to his rooms. It gets worse each time, I don't fancy him any more. I try to disguise it, but…"

"Well, you can't help going off someone if you don't see him often enough," Emma sagely commented from her adjacent computer, missing the point completely.

Louise had to think of a backing-out plan, but first she needed to make sure that Harry would remember her in his will. Careful questioning ferreted out that he had indeed provided some legacy for her, but he would not divulge how much. There was not much else she could do. She was cornered. Carl was coming round this weekend, a healthy young builder that she had met via work. They usually met in a different pub not far from the flat.

She thought of different ways all day at work and came home to make diagrams and plans again and again until the main outline of action emerged. Louise bought a blonde wig, an inconspicuous mac, plain flat shoes. Wearing the new outfit, she searched out an industrial outfitters, buying a chambermaid's black overall and apron that matched the Bay Tree House uniform. The premises were across in Elephant and Castle, but she took the caution of wearing a different red wig and glasses. Over her jacket, she wore a second-hand camel-hair coat which she discarded in a clothing bank on the way home.

Harry would be waiting at Bay Tree House in his suite which took up all the top floor. It was the best apartment in the hotel, with views all over the city's changing skyline. He was always particular about being punctual. Louise, dressed as one of the chambermaids, darted up the back emergency stairs, a towel over her arm, hiding a knife. Knocking on his door, he would merely be both amused and a bit puzzled at her changed appearance. But the CCTV records would merely show a blonde maid calling with extra laundry. Once in the room, Louise managed to stab him several times as rapidly as possible, fear of being discovered giving her an extra frantic power. Harry's surprised face was the last memory she would have of him, as he crumpled onto the thick carpet, clutching to the low chair beside the bed. Within a few minutes she had left the suite as she had arrived, hurrying down the back stairs to the yard at the back of the kitchens. If anyone saw her, they saw a maid with blonde hair.

Behind the hotel's tall rubbish bins in the yard she had already managed to hide a plain grey coat and a dark brown wig, all in a plastic shopping bag. Switching wigs, placing the apron, towel and knife in the bag and putting on the grey coat, Louise stole out of the hotel's back yard looking nondescript and walked towards the main road, strolling down the back streets trying to avoid any CCTV cameras.

At home she swiftly burned the two wigs, the coat and towel (both torn up into pieces) and even put the knife into the fire to remove as much trace of blood as possible. There would be no trace of the disguise to link with her. Next morning going out to work, she dropped the knife, with its burnt handle, down a drain along a deserted suburban road and hoped for the best.

All Harry's years of carefully constructed successful deceit of his wife would add to her security. He had kept the two parts of his life clearly separate. There was no trace of any of the links between them, except his will. That could be explained away by pretending to be a devoted secretary from when he first set up his business.

The only other snag was Carl complaining about the dreadful smell in the flat when he turned up on Sunday.

Louise waited impatiently for the will to come out of probate. Harry had left her only a few hundred pounds and the deeds to the flat. She was mentioned as a loyal former secretary, as expected. Stifling her disappointment, Louise took the best pieces of her jewellery collection to a shop for valuation, with excitement. There was the Pari Patek watch and the pagoda diamond ring after all, with some other pieces in their velvet-lined boxes.

"I am so sorry," the jeweller said, as he spread them out carefully on the green felt cloth. "You won't get much for these. Magnificent pieces, certainly, but they are not worth much at all. They are all counterfeit, it's the very best Hong Kong work, admirable, in fact it's the best in the world. A very shrewd purchase on someone's part, I would venture to say," he congratulated her as she left. The double row of pearls was the only genuine item and she got eighty pounds for them, not caring to haggle for any more.

Louise could remember Harry coming back in triumph from his business visits to Hong Kong and the Far East and how pleased she had been when he produced those gifts from abroad. Perhaps the *Joy* perfume had been fake too, but it was far too late to find that out and with the aggressive new movement against animal cruelty, the mink coat was now unwearable in public.

Two Saturdays

The planning meeting had been boring, as expected, but perhaps this time it was even worse. They could not change official policy much, even if a meeting was successful. They were like parties without the drink, dancing or music and just like parties, one thing led to another. Ban this, save this, print posters, send off letters, sign petitions, arrange another meeting, plan a demo or a procession and repeat, repeat. It was a relief to get out into the cool of the April night.

She moved quickly away from the hall, not wanting to be collared to give out leaflets or have a dozen posters to put up round town. If Ken knew you did not help out enough, you would be cold-shouldered; not exactly exiled, but the same effect. There was still that dozen leaflets that she had not delivered last month. She hoped Ken had not noticed. Jim offered her a lift home, but she knew he was rather clingy and it might end up in an embarrassing situation and said,

"Thanks a lot but I'll walk home and think things out on the way. It's a lovely night. Goodbye!" She wandered back through town, thinking all this over – perhaps she could still put those leaflets through people's front doors? They would throw them away, being out of date but at least she could say it had been done, problem solved.

It was late now and right on closing time. Town was different when all the shops were closed. In the silence the canvas roofs of the market stalls flapping echoed across. She detoured through the market now. Stalls shuttered for the night still let out clues to what they sold. The tang of oranges, the sharp whiff of onions – she could guess each one as she passed by. And now, there were footsteps behind her, definitely. Taking a side-cut, the footsteps followed her. It was the copycat of any film noir, the endless alleys of shuttered stalls, the tap-tap of feet, the creak of beams as the canvases flapped here and there in the wind. Whoever it was, followed her carefully, going after her every move as she switched side-alleys.

Only last Saturday the market was entirely different, right in the middle of an extraordinary and violent thunderstorm. Bolts of lightning and the onslaught of heavy rain meant people were stranded in the market, dashing under the awnings for shelter. Shoppers huddled under any sheltered corner and passed the time buying chips or anything that was available. Children were suddenly able to choose any toy to pass the time.

In the midst of the cloudburst, a very posh lady said loudly

"But it's only a shower!" Except her accent made it 'a shaaah!' People stared and giggled. They waited as the heavy rains continued pouring down, thudding on the canvas or shed roofs. Floods streamed down the alleyways and along the end gulley like a small Niagra. Drips of water cascaded dangerously down the electric light fixtures, but luckily nothing exploded. Stallholders

26

continued selling goods as if it was a normal Saturday, and with people trapped and unwilling to chance going off into that teeming rain, trade was really good.

And just as suddenly the downpour ended and a surprising spring sunshine appeared, as rain steamed up from the warm pavements. One by one people shuffled off – they dispersed happily, bags of fruit and veg in their grasp. The unsettled spring weather was here at last.

And now it was another clear night, with the calm that spreads after a stormy week. No distractions, the clarity of streets when no one was shopping, left as a town planner's neat drawing. Only shop lights here and there, with smaller premises having no lights at all. Side-streets were dark as she walked past Tesco's, its shopping trollies all neatly nestled into each other. The taxi rank had a few idling cabs, their drivers still on duty.

It must have been about then that she noticed the footsteps behind her were still pacing regularly and, unlike the few people who were about, never actually passing her by. She had stopped and looked at the bookshop window, its glossy covers of coffee-table books as enticing as boxes of chocolates – there had been no one around the street then. The footsteps had stopped.

Next, she went past a roughish sort of pub that no one she knew had ever gone into. Strange that, how there was a secret hierarchy of pubs which outsiders would not know about. But the footsteps were definitely a regular rhythm behind her again, now, past the futon shop, the stationery shop, some offices and a chained-up carpark.

No one was walking towards her, and while there was someone on the opposite pavement, he might help. Or would he? How can you trust one man to rescue you from another? It could end up worse, with the new man insisting on seeing her home – and how to get away from *him* then? There were no women about at all. She was the only one. Should have accepted that lift from Jim after all.

The classic advice in these situations was for the woman to cross the road – but soon they were in a cul-de-sac leading to a footbridge over the main road. She would only have to cross over again, right into the path of this follower. Luckily, at the end of this group of townhouses and shut shops was a small pub, The Queen's Head. A sign of an almost-smiling Queen Victoria shone a welcome across the empty street.. Should she go in there, buy an orange juice and play for time? But it would be silly to enter a very small pub at closing time and expect to be ignored or left alone. What about going in there and saying she was being followed and ask for help? Surely that would be like putting her head into a lion's mouth and not expecting it to bite? A pub-full of white knights, all kindly disposed and preferably sober with honourable and protective instincts at closing time? If anything went wrong, the police, the newspapers and the neighbours would all blame her. No, she wold have to go on and think of something else, desperate. But there were less and less choices now.

The footsteps went on and on, mimicking her every step. If she slowed down, he slowed down too, and did not pass her; if she hurried up, he speeded up too. It was as if he was making fun of her, in a horrible way.

There was only the arched footbridge in sight now, which led to a clump of overgrown bushes, a patch of 'amenity planting' that some planner had thought was a good idea but was perfect for sheltering from any passer-by or traffic in its dense undergrowth. A wonderful place for muggers, in fact there was often a discarded purse or wallet left among the litter of crisp packets and drink cans.

But there was a larger pub nestled there, right beside the footbridge's slope down to the other pavement.. If she ran the last bit through the shrubbery and right into the pub, she could phone up from there for a taxi home. It would take all the week's food money but it would be an escape. Strange, how when you are trapped you can come up with a solution, however extreme. So, setting up the slope to the arching footbridge, a midget version of the Sydney Harbour Bridge, she felt more confident. But the footsteps drew nearer and nearer. He drew level with her – and strolled by. He was small, in his forties, probably an office worker, balding, with glasses, wearing a long thick black coat even on a night like this and carrying a briefcase. He was not even much taller than herself. In fact he looked tired, a bit stooped-over.

Giddy with relief, she wanted to run up and put her hand on his shoulder and ask him what on earth did he think he was playing at?

"I thought you were going to attack me!" He had obviously enjoyed the thrill of stalking her but for some reason had changed his mind at the last minute. What had caused the change? He strode off, along the bridge into the night and disappeared along the main road towards the hulking cathedral. Perhaps he got a thrill out of doing this often. Cars passed below them down the hill.

She was overcome with joy now and started to sing. The stars were sharp, distinct up here, with no roofs to hide the sky. She wandered past the last pub – which had its doors closed already, and walked happily along what might have been more dangerous parts where the churchyard lay, dark and featureless. Still singing and delighting in the beautiful spring night she passed long gardens, houses with few lights on at this late hour and dark side streets full of parked cars.

Nearing home, past a row of shops, she could hear someone whistling, as if they were calling a dog to heel. A swish beside her, and looking down, expecting a red setter because that was her favourite dog, she saw instead a be-jeaned leg and then looking up saw a young man smiling at her. Even in this dark she could see he was sunburnt, handsome, tall, blond and blue-eyed.

"I thought you'd never stop!" he said, laughing. "Didn't you hear me?" She heard the trace of a Great Yarmouth accent, softer than their inland accents. "I'd just been up to the all-night garage for milk and ciggies."

"I thought you were calling a dog to heel," she said, laughing too.

"I live right up there," he pointed to a top window of a large Victorian house. "And you can call round if you'd like." He started to talk about Buddhism and getting rid of belongings and clutter. "You can re-design your own life, if you try." Face to face, an effortless encounter. How different this was, ludicrous, just the two of them alone here in the night street, standing holding hands and laughing. No one was around. She told him she lived nearby and so he said he could call round soon with some books on philosophy if she was interested.

"My room's full of books, you'd be surprised." And so Phil picked her up, as anyone would have called it, and she inexplicably fell in love right there in the middle of the street. But she did not get round to telling him, ever, about the man who had followed her mercilessly. He was forgotten. There was no way she could have explained to anyone the crucial difference here, the lack of risk; not something that can be measured, except it is instantaneous, like lightning.

The Wife of Bath

There's always someone like this on a coach trip and she *would* end up sitting next to me. A middle aged or well-preserved woman, startling henna-dyed hair, lots of jewellery and those long imitation nails that show you don't do any housework. And of course she had been everywhere, even as far as Jerusalem.

Not short of money either. Five husbands, the latest one in his twenties and she was forty if she was a day. The breeze of expensive perfume drifted past.

"Call me Ally," she said. "I only use Alison for anything official." She had such a gale of friendliness that I couldn't draw back. I sat back, well, there was no escape and decided to give in and just listen. It was a long journey to Canterbury; we were doing a tour of cathedrals, with an overnight stop here and there. Of course I would end up sharing a room with Ally – how do you stop a hurricane like that. And it was only a kindness to keep her away from any of the men, or husband number six would have drifted into sight and been immediately boarded.

Ally was confident in all her opinions. She started to give me, as a younger woman, all the benefits of her philosophy and experience. As I wanted only one husband, not five or more, any tip would have been welcome. She oozed confidence as well as perfume. "My first marriage was when I was a teenager, those were the days. And you know, I'm just the same as that Samaritan woman that Jesus met at the well – she had five … not exactly husbands, in fact he told her off about that, just like an older brother would do. But then, a lot of the Old Testament guys, like Abraham, – and look at Solomon! - they all had lots of wives, lots and lots.

I mean, you start off as a virgin, but if everyone stayed like that the world would be empty." Ally looked pointedly across at a nun and her little companion, both probably certified virgins, sitting on the seats across the aisle. "The fathers of the church don't think that out properly." I wondered what the nun and the nun's companion and the young probationer would say about all this. Probably best I kept them apart. "As a young woman, you've got this sexual power, you find out all about that soon enough and then you go on to use it to control your husband, that's what I say," she smiled benignly. "My first three husbands were no trouble at all, well, they were quite old and easily manoeuvred, and rich!"

She told me she used to taunt them that they were having an affair or if they got drunk she would make up what they had said to make them feel bad the next day. And then taking advantage of their guilt, she would wheedle some present out of them. She would tease them in bed, holding the poor things off at the very brink of satisfaction until they promised her money.

Two of the husbands, however, she said were 'bad' meaning they were not entirely under her thumb. Her fourth husband was a drinker and party-goer and he also acquired a mistress, which showed that Alison was starting to lose her looks and power over him. He died, most conveniently, while she was on the pilgrimage to Jerusalem. But now she was madly in love with her fifth husband, Jacob. She said she fell in love with him when she saw him carrying her husband's coffin. He was a student who was lodging at the time with a friend of hers in the village.

But her confidence in her sexiness was waning and this young Jacob would not put up with her dramatics like the others. His youth gave him the advantage. In one of their fights she punched him in the face and he hit her so hard that she became deaf in one ear. It was all about Jacob coming home one night with copies of *Loaded* and *Big Girls*. Alison tore pages out of the magazines, threw them onto the floor and punched him in the face.

She did not say if he was still alive and out of tactfulness I did not ask. When we got off the coach that afternoon I drifted off and took care not to sit next to her again. Poor Mr Pardoner, who was getting married soon sat next to her the next part of the trip and I wonder what terrible thoughts were going through his mind as Alison rambled on with this amazing tale of out-of-control marriages.

She reminded me of another rich American woman on a retreat I went to, at a monastery over one Lent. That American woman also had heavy perfume, lots of clanking gold jewellery, long red nails and very low-cut blouses. She flirted madly with the Benedictine monks, to the obvious embarrassment of one young monk. Young enough to be her son, Brother Claude was trying to start a discussion on "What is Love?" with this lady's distracting bosom drawing nearer and nearer, to his growing discomfort, causing him to stutter and lose his place.

As we said our farewells at Southwark Cathedral and Alison wandered down the road to London Bridge station for the train back to Bath, I thought how her worldliness and religious fervour intertwined so closely that they could not be undone from each other. I left thinking about this rogue vagabond of a woman and if she might be heaven-bound before the lot of us, with her wild innocence.

"God bade us to wax fruitful and multiply," She trundled off with her wheeled suitcase rattling over the cobbles, like a force of nature.

I am rather too believing and perhaps naïve, as my friends pointed out when I told them about the pilgrimage and the other travellers, especially Alison.

"Four dead husbands?" Malcolm nearly fell off the sofa. "And no body'd cottoned on yet? That Jacob's had a luck escape then, hope he moves out while the going's good and stays with the landlady, he's far safer. The woman's a serial killer, that's why she goes on pilgrimages; it's a good cover story."

He was right, once I'd thought it over, but I couldn't face going to the police and the papers about it. Perhaps it was all made up, and Alison was really a sad old maid with a fervid imagination. That's what I said to Malcolm and we went off to the pub. That was years ago and I've never ever gone on a pilgrimage since.

Chapel Lane

For some time now Jim Grogan had been worried about his field that was increasingly edged by houses. He did not own the land at the top of the slope and had to put up with all the diggers and contraptions that mulched up the soil as the housing estate grew day after day. New house-owners rapidly moved in and from then on he felt as though every window, curtained, or with French blinds, Austrian drapes or whatever, held someone watching him as he walked across his land with his dog.

For several years now he had rented it out to Eamon Keogh, who grew onions for a food factory in Sligo, manufacturing chutneys and crisps. By the time of the autumn harvest the entire district smelled like a large bag of crisps.

"Who's eating crisps on this bus?" a pernickety pensioner would ask as the four-a-day local bus sailed past the field. "Why don't they take the empty packets home with them! Litter louts!" And so it would go on, year after year. And then old man Keogh died and it turned out that his son was not interested in farming any more.

"Yes, I know it's a surprise. Sorry, won't be renewing the contract on the field, I'm going in for tropical fish, that's always been my hobby. Just tagged along with dad, had to. Sad he's gone and all, but there's Mum to think of as well, she's in a bit of a state too, you see." Jim Grogan had not made any specific leasing arrangement and so it looked as though he would have to find a new tenant for next year in a hurry. No one was interested in renting a single field surrounded by new houses. Even the advantage of having Cleary's pub right at the corner of the lane made no difference.

Cleary said he did not mind if the field was used for keeping horses, they were more picturesque to look at than any onion sets. But the weeks flew past and no one appeared. While quite abstemious, Jim still needed some income and was getting desperate. The first snows arrived and the field was wiped clean with just the rim of houses breaking the skyline. So when the phone call came one evening he was only too eager to agree to a new tenant moving in.

"It's the field at the edge of the main road, isn't it? Just interested to see I've got the right place after all."

"Yes, just past the bus stop and Cleary's pub is on the corner, you can't miss it."

The new tenant, Basil, had no quibbles about the rent and paid three months' worth in cash as deposit right away. He arrived with his wife, a black-haired beauty dressed in a flowing multi-coloured dress. In fact Basil and Rhona were both hippyish, but all the better, Jim thought, as people like them were always interested in anything to do with land and agriculture.

"Not sure yet which crop to set, lots to think over before spring, you know what it's like," Basil said breezily, "Sugar beet's been rather overdone round here and I noticed that there's not as much rapeseed as there was a couple of years ago, fashion or trade, you never really know. We keep a few horses over Fortfield way too, and Rhona's family have small market garden, they supply a few of the farm shops in the county. This is amazing, we're lucky it's such a convenient situation, couldn't have asked for anything better." And so it was settled and Jim ambled into Cleary's and had a lone celebratory drink, not telling the few locals there that evening anything about the new arrangement.

Nothing happened until summer approached, when a faint red bloom spread across the field. But soon one further red bloom showed up after another and it was soon obvious the field was becoming covered with poppies. Its shocking bright scarlet splash of colour stood out from the usual plain humble green of other surrounding crops in the district and the houses sited on the skyline were like toys left out after a child's bedtime. People started to talk about it. The bus driver was surprised at first, then he noticed more passengers and more hikers appearing. News spread about the scarlet field and photographers and then artists flocked to the scene. They stayed for drinks in the pub and swapped tips about paint techniques. Various artists' groups arrived from nearby counties by the coachload.

Local publicity magazine journalists turned up too. One of them contacted the local radio station, who had to admit it was wasted on mere radio and it was definitely a made-for-TV spectacle. Prizewinning photographers took photos for future calendars and birthday cards. Soon the poppy field was on Facebook and established internationally. Local artists had a new impetus and many previously bored painters came out and started to paint enthusiastically again. Exhibitions showed walls full of brightly-hued poppies in close-up or as a wide sweep of red. Only Jim Grogan was angry. He knew the field was ruined, not just by this invasion of tourists to Chapel Lane, but because the poppy seeds would be in the ground forever and could turn up again in the midst of another crop.

The art supplies shop in the nearest town had soon run out of vermilion, cadmium red and had even managed to shift tubes of the less safe carmine, scarlet lake, crimson lake, geranium lake and even rose madder and magenta.

"And you know," the shopkeeper said, "Red is a fugitive colour, it can change dramatically and it's not always stable. It can fade, the hue will completely disappear and ruin a painting if you're not careful. It's almost the same cycle, really, you could say it's like a poppy field in a tube."

Tuesday Nights

On the way back from work, winter evening, rain sleeting down. Ben walked up the hill from town. Not too far to go now. Not much to look forward to. Change out of these sopping clothes and wet shoes, have a cup of coffee and start the weekend. Very little money left, no spectacular going-out on Saturday night, just like all the others.

But he had to get through this Friday night first. And it was as he passed the video shop for the umpteenth time, that a change of mind led him to step through the shabby doorway, looking for something cheap to distract him. He passed along the shelves, past The Sound of Music and other family-friendly films, past the sci-fi and horror flics to the classics like The Third Man.

A further shelf, labelled Film Noir, intrigued him and after a quick search he took One Way Street, a 1950s James Mason film that had stolen money, gangs, guns, gunman's moll and an idyllic Mexican Village interlude. Black and white films had always intrigued him and he settled down to an evening's entertainment. Saturday night, it was the pub as usual, starting from the aptly named M.T.Pockets up Prospect Hill. Drink, friends, chat, other pubs, party, drunk, home somehow; the usual weekend, and back to work on Monday as the stupor wore off.

Ben had to return the video during the week and called in for another one.

"If you're that interested," the lanky guy behind the counter said, "There's an evening class at the Uni up the road, all about film noir. It's free to city residents, you just have to give your name at the door." He produced a handout. Tuesday evenings. Yes, almost midweek, no money left and another wait for the weekend. "You get our videos half-price if you join the course, too."

It was Ben's first walk through the university entrance. He had sometimes used the grounds as a quick cut-through on his bike, but had never gone inside the buildings. The porter at the stone-built gatehouse gave him the instructions,

"Just through the quadrangle and it's the first door on the right. There'll be a sign on the lecture hall, 'Film Noir' or something like that." And so Ben sidled into a back row of the hall, finding a seat and looking down at the screen and the lecturer. At nine p.m. he came out again, his head awhirl with titles, themes, stars' names as well as writers, directors and producers, plus a large dollop of social history.

Luckily the enthusiastic lecturer gave out A4 sheets of titles to look out for. As they collected this information, he noticed a girl with emerald green eyes and wondered how he could get into conversation with her. Dropping his notes, he managed to get in her way along the corridor and started right there.

"What did you think of all that?" She said it was good to see a messy group of films all put into order,

"So we can work our way through it easily." A few nights later Ben introduced Sandra to the video shop he used on the way home. The owner was delighted at the extra custom.

"You get it at reduced price because of the course, it's win-win all round – the university gets more grants for reaching out to local townspeople, and we get more trade. Less Disney films out and more of your old, classic black and whites."

Ben became eaten up by two parallel things – Sandra and the films. He took to wearing sunglasses at all times possible, only removing them at the laundry offices where he worked, chasing up bills to local hotels and residential institutions. The dark glasses transformed everything - changed forever, his humdrum surroundings into one long, if rather dull film noir.

He was obsessed with Sandra now and managed to get her to walk along to the video shop with him after each meeting. She was not very talkative but he hardly noticed. Things were going well, Ben thought, though it was obvious that their only point of contact was the evening classes – only three more to go –and they had nothing more in common. He would definitely ask her out for a drink next time. And suddenly Sandra vanished. She did not turn up at the university any more. He asked the lecturer, who was rather vague about her and was not interested.

"She was not a regular student here, she was like yourself, just a casual attender – if you don't mind my saying so – from town." Ben became frantic. How could he find her? She had given no clues to her address or who she lived with. He realised at his late stage, that he did not know if she had a boyfriend or shared a flat with anyone or lived at home still. He was surprised, now, how little he knew about Sandra at all. She had hinted that she worked in a bank, but there were several in town and very few counter clerks these days. He could try asking round the banks on a Saturday morning, perhaps.

He was on his way back home one evening, sunglasses on even in the early evening rain. As he was going past the video shop he had a bright idea at last. They had to give names and addresses to hire videos. He could ask the guy behind the counter for her address. Problem solved.

But the gawky lad claimed professional discretion.

"It's the data act. We are not allowed to share data, private information and all that. We'd lose our licence to trade. Sorry about that."

"You don't look sorry," Ben said, aggrieved. The images crowded round and Ben saw the video shop assistant as the sole person who could complete his life, who was here, right now, standing in his way. He could not move on from this at all. He began to call into the shop at all hours, to chide and plead with the guy, who he found out was called Dean. That was all.

He waited outside the shop late one November evening, determined to get the address once and for all, but Dean was not answering. Ben pushed Dean aside as he was locking up. He was amazed at his own power, Ben was fuming, this guy had no clue about his fears and frustrations. The pit of all the violence he had taken in had become part of his psyche. And now he was in the midst of his own film as Dean struggled away from him and, running out into the road to escape, was thumped by a car coming down the hill. The sound was authentic this time, that ominous crunch of bone against ground. The black rain fell down his sunglasses as he walked up the hill towards home. People had come out of the nearby houses as the police and an ambulance appeared. He was the innocent bystander, a necessity in these cases.

Three weeks to go on the course and now he was in his own film noir narrative, just like the end of that One Way Street film, his very first rental, where James Mason was killed by a car in the rain. That film ended with the girl-friend weeping as the police arrived.

Ben had been asked to go to the police station tomorrow in his lunch hour to make a statement, though of course the poor motorist would get the blame. He could make up a different ending for them all, if he liked. He knew all about how to structure a narrative now.

Chocolate Murders

It was interesting to sit here in the airport. Pisa airport was smallish, but did have the usual array of shops and cafés, with an escalator up to an extra layer of shops. Tessa wandered around for a while but seeing a row of seats, made for them, to have a rest.

Stopping at the general store, she was already stocked with another bottle of spring water to cope with the heat. It was amazing to see the display of cigarettes spread behind the counter. For a couple of years now it had been forbidden in England to show any cigarettes for sale. They were always hidden behind sliding cupboard doors and a customer had to ask particularly, humbly, if they wanted to purchase any packet of cigarettes.

Her friend, Moira who worked at the Co-op, said that if the sliding doors were open even slightly, the shop would get fined £4,000. It looked as though different rules were obeyed or broken in the EU, as here in Italy surely the same rules existed. It was all a mess of decisions criss-crossing each other.

The young woman sitting next to her was engrossed in her phone, a private existence in a public space. Beside her were two large suitcases wreathed tightly in layers of bright light-green plastic, almost phosphorescent.

A young man stood in the middle of the concourse, a Green Wrap hero with his bolts of plastic, and a contraption ready to festoon any baggage with green wrapping. Once done, it looked so complete that the traveller would not be able to open their luggage without unweaving all the layers. What on earth did the silent girl have in those two cases, or was she going through several stopovers and needed extra security?

Tessa, bored now, went off for another walk round the corridors and deposited her own small suitcase through the baggage handlers' counters. As she walked back, the same seat was empty so she sat down again in the same place.

Suddenly the girl turned to her and with a warm smile offered Tessa some chocolate. It was the end of the bar, a couple of broken segments in the silver-paper wrapper. They introduced themselves. Gina was from Argentina and on her way to Spain to visit her sister. Tessa said she was going back to England after visiting relatives on holiday in Florence.

"I've got to write a murder story for a writers' group by next week and you've given me an idea. This chocolate could be poisoned and there would be no trace of how it happened. Of course there could be CCTV of us here now, but I can't see any cameras. I think there's some rule that they have to be observable if it's a public place or perhaps that's an urban myth. But thank you."

Tessa wandered outside to throw away the remains of her bottle of water before going through passport control. Outside in the humid heat, two young soldiers stood on duty. She asked if it was all right to throw the water onto a potted plant and the dark-haired soldier signalled yes. The bush would need some water today, surely. She slung the plastic bottle into the nearby rubbish bin and that was the last she saw of Italy. The trademark dark plumed Italian trees were far away beyond the humdrum layout of the airport buildings and its carpark.

Back home, Tessa looked up poisonous plants and remembered laburnum, and sure, there it was. All parts of the plant were (or are) poisonous although mortality could be rare. Symptoms of laburnum poisoning included intense sleepiness, vomiting, convulsive movements, coma, frothing at the mouth and, the reference said, unequally dilated pupils. Who would notice that in the midst of all the other signs?

Tessa set to work. This information was far too exciting to waste time on mere writing. Along the suburban lane on the way to the park, a magnificent laburnum tree swept over the wall of an old mansion waiting for redevelopment. Its long trails of bright yellow flowerets could be seen from afar; it was always a sign of late spring. She waited until the seedpods were formed and picked several when no one was about.

Buying some bars of dark chocolate, with their strong, almost bitter taste, she melted the bars, folding in the ground-up seeds. Leaving the lot to set, she had to think out the next step. In some of the crime books she had read, a poisoner tried out their doses on something smaller like a cat or dog. Wasn't it in the Bywaters and Thompson murder, Florence, the wife who had also given the husband a mild dose at first, gradually increasing the amount weekly? Mixed in with a stew or fish and chips or cheese on toast it would have been well disguised. There was some sort of medical protocol that if a person had been unwell for some time, and if that person had been seen by a doctor in the week previous to their death, then an inquest would not be necessary.

Tessa of course could not embark on such a slow process with any strangers. But a small experiment with next-door's cat was amazingly successful. She tried to look upset on learning that the fat malevolent moggy had been taken seriously ill. It had died before the vet had been able to arrive as there was a violent thunderstorm at the time.

"Perhaps it was heart failure?" Tessa said airily. "We don't know how animals react in the middle of a thunderstorm, they must get affected. When I was a child our dog always hid under one of the fireside chairs and wouldn't come out until it was all over."

She made another batch, upping the amount of laburnum seeds. Somewhere in the past, perhaps in the sixth form, they had studied George Orwell's *The Decline of the English Murder*. He had suggested that when divorce was unobtainable in the lower classes, domestic poisonings were the only way out for discontented wives (usually the wife) or husbands. While some, stupidly in fact, went to a chemist's and asked for arsenic to kill rats, other, cleverer ones collected poisonous innocent-looking plants like foxglove or laburnum. Those who bought arsenic from chemists' shops had to sign a Poisons Book, which was one of the first things police would inspect. But few police could trace a walk down a country lane and some leaves or seeds gathered into a bag or pocket.

With her new pensioner's bus pass, Tessa went off to Heathrow and arrived full of enthusiasm. The new red wig and glasses gave a carefully different image. She found a seat in one of the waiting lounges and offered some chocolate to the first person who sat next to her. It was a pity, though, that she would not find out what happened until someone cottoned on to the number of people passing through the airport waiting section were eventually dying of poison. She would be clever enough to stop then, once it hit the newspapers.

Extra-Special Event

Late Friday afternoon, the coach trundled along the country lanes, riotously festooned with weeds, Leonard noticed. He was trying to keep from being too friendly too soon, but assumed that all the other people on the coach were also going to Fallowbrook Village. The large, loud lady, or was she merely a woman? He wondered at that demarcation line, sat in front loudly chatting to a small quiet woman. Then there was the intense, almost resentful older man who clutched a small carry-case on his knee and who had not spoken to anyone yet, much like himself. Perhaps the others were locals who had been off to the big city for shopping, like true country bumpkins.

In all, Leonard thought, it's like the beginning of an Agatha Christie novel, where a gang of strangers, or more likely an extremely polite group to start with, are gathered together in a minor stately home and something goes rotten in the woodwork. He was already on his guard.

At least the setting was right – Old Fallowbrook Hall was certainly impressive, with stone balconies and terraces and a massive carved oaken front door. The place had been left by a rich composer, to be used as a centre for aspiring artists, writers and musicians so they could have hideaway time in order to create. Richard Offay had made a fortune writing theme music for films and this was a way round the entire place being left to a distant relative in Canada or eaten up in Capital Gains tax.

To make it even better, the centre issued generous bursaries, which was how Leonard, recently retired and increasingly aimless, had ended up here as a writer. It was a chance of a month's free board and lodging without having to do much for it. The writing he had sent in as proof was actually his dead sister's. Agnes had always stayed at home, looking after their mother until Mrs Reedham had died almost two years ago. The endless days had been spent writing interminable sagas that were never fully resolved, but now they were worth their weight in gold.

Leonard was launched on the public as a published writer without the Fallowbrook organisers finding out the deceit. He had sent poor Agnes' shorter pieces out to online sites under his own name; an easy thing to do. There were reams and reams of her stuff; he would never need to write anything again, ever. Old Mrs Reedham's kitchen dresser, her sideboard, even her dressing table had been stuffed with poor Agnes's outpourings and trilogies, while Agnes's own room was almost a fire-risk of gathered papers and notebooks. He only had to type the lot out on his new computer, bit by bit. Leonard was made for life now.

Friday evening they assembled in Fallowbrook Hall's dining room for their first official dinner. This was one of the rules. Amazingly (the place must be rolling in money, Leonard thought,) there was a resident staff to cater for them and be on call when needed. In his casting around for somewhere like this, Leonard found that other centres made the inmates do the cooking and washing up. There was no host; here the guests had to introduce themselves; there was no convenor or facilitator, nothing modern like that. Names had to be repeated or spelled out. The ratty-faced man turned out to be a composer, with his life's work clutched in a satchel; the loud woman was a textile designer, the quiet woman was writing a book on yoga, a spritely young thing was designing a model city, while a reserved young man was compiling a catalogue of thimbles. The others did not say much and Leonard was at the other end of the table. He was content for them to remain a mystery, like himself.

But Rita, the loud woman, had been here before.

"Oh yes, you can come here at least three times before they get a bit squiffy about you. I get such a boost for new designs, I can tell you. By the way, you know the village Fête is on tomorrow? We could all go and have a bit of fun!"

The ratty-faced composer sniffed that there would be the usual oompha oompha brass band disturbing all the birds. But the quiet yoga woman, Lydia, said surely the crass medley would inspire him to write his own stuff even better, in contrast? The girl designing model cities (now in the plural) said it was imperative to study the population of villages and extrapolate from that to mega-city size.

"We are programmed to relate to about two-hundred people. After that it gets a bit hazy and beyond a thousand, human interaction fades away, genuine care, that is." She looked sad as though Fallowbrook Village had let the world down by having several dozen surplus inhabitants.

So it was decided that just like lords of the manor, they would descend on the village after lunch and survey the scene and the people. Being such independent and unsociable people themselves, they soon separated and wandered round amongst the merry but controlled mayhem. Everything was all as it should be in the classic English country fair. Stalls of home-made cakes and jams next to stalls of bric-a-brac, a white elephant stall, a fortune teller's tent, a bouncy castle, an Aunt Sally wet sponge shy, a plate-shooting gallery, a guess the weight stand, second hand books and a few rails of second-hand clothes. Carts and vans sold ice cream, pancakes and candy floss in fluorescent pink.

They wandered about, being superior and eying it as if it was a film set. Each of them was taking an aspect to use back at Fallowbrook Hall.

And then it happened. A vast whirlwind descended, taking up clothes from the rails, books from the shelves, china and ornaments from the bric-a-brac stall. A candy floss floated off into the sky like a merry cloud. Anything not tethered securely was taken into the small tornado and whisked up into the sky. Books and cutlery mixed above them with floating scarves and trousers. Stout wellington boots separated and fell apart into different fields after whirling about in the air. For what had been taken up so rapidly had been discarded by whatever force had made it rise, and now the objects were returning to earth rapidly, in no particular order.

Children were crying as they were hit by copies of old books like Sesame and Lilies, or even worse, a volume of Arthur Mee's Children's Encyclopaedia. Cups, teapots and plates smashed as they landed from a great height. Like a hippy's dream, various pieces of clothing crossed with each other overhead and returned to earth entwined as if romantically. Large cardboard boxes landed on some people's heads, blinding them for a moment. Dogs ran about barking, trying to defend the field. A couple of the tents lost parts of their panels and people were running away as fast as they could, back home where their own roof was still on.

The vicar could see his next Sunday's service being his very best, one founded on a good quote from the Old Testament, God at his retributive best. *The Last Judgement, Heaven and Hell,* something like that. No nice soft Jesus stuff for a change. Any sinners in the village must be having a change of heart right now.

The creatives from Fallowbrook Hall looked on at the event, somehow unmoved and saw only wonderfully unique material for their next projects.

Hotel Curtains

It was early spring and I was staying in a small guesthouse in Vienna. It was annoying, I found the morning light woke me up early each day. These places always have thin curtains so their guests are not tempted to stay in bed too long, and have to appear on time for early breakfast. A formal "Good morning" to the other guests was enough to start the day. I never knew how people managed to meet accidentally. I never met anyone by chance, ever. I did not know how it was done.

And so, a couple of days on this solo trip to Austria, it was without really realising it that I 'met' Rudi Beck. He must have sidled up to me in the street, just after I came out of a small antique shop. It was skilfully done, looking back at that first encounter. I was really pleased with myself, for handling it so politely.

"Ah, you are interested in antiques?" he asked, smiling. "Well, I know of a wonderful place somewhere along by the Donaukanal," he said. And I found myself walking along the streets with him as we started chatting about how various pieces catch your eye and you start to hanker after them. He knew all the side streets in Vienna and all the short cuts. "You'll be really surprised at what you'll find here, it's exceptional, a real treasure-trove," he said, in perfect English. We were well past the Votivkirche by now. "I've known this place for years, it always turns up bargains. You are lucky to have met me, I can introduce you here, it will make all the difference."

Rudi knocked at the shabby door and we waited until an elderly woman opened the door a few inches and peered at us. She spoke to him as if she was annoyed, but began to smile when she saw me.

We entered a cluttered and neglected junkshop, though that would be perhaps a cruel way to describe it. There were pieces here that were probably worth a small fortune, carved chests and chairs that looked as though they had been purloined from Austrian castles way up in the mountains. They were all well beyond my funds. But I bought a small writing case, inlaid with mother of pearl and lined with green velvet, now faded and stained. It would be easy to carry back to where I was staying. Rudi and the old woman were pleased and Rudi surprisingly suggested we go for a drink together later on. He invited me to his flat for later that evening. We could decide where to go on from there, he suggested.

I had heard that there were situations where girls inveigled men to come back to their flat for sex, only for the mark to be mugged and beaten up at the top of the stairs by her accomplices. I was not going to fall for a variation on something like that. No one knew where I was. No, I said to Rudi, it would not be a good idea, what about meeting somewhere else? I was becoming increasingly suspicious of him.

"Oh, but I have some wonderful pieces you would be interested in," he said. "There are some real

Meissen figurines, obviously, you'll really appreciate them, someone like yourself is so wonderful to meet, a fellow collector." So I agreed to it, with some misgivings. He gave me the address and directions on how to get there. We parted at the entrance to the Steigenberger Hotel.

His flat was well beyond the Naschmarkt, past a small group of residential buildings and set in a street of empty offices. At eight in the evening, few people were still about. The distant bells from St Stephen's cathedral rang out the hour exactly.

Rudi had set out the decanter, glasses and a tray of small biscuits, he was very organised. I already knew he lived alone and was not expecting anyone else to turn up. We sat and drank the rich deep port, watching the sunset stream through the long windows that reached from floor to ceiling. He waffled on about parts of Austrian history and went on and on without stopping.

It was so easy to attack his unsuspecting head with the heavy wrought iron antique doorstop and see him collapse down on the carpet. No need to kill him, just enough to put him out long enough to make my escape. I had already noticed which pocket he kept his wallet in and quickly removed all the notes. The second we had entered his crowded flat, with a rapid view round the room I had easily identified any valuable small pieces. There were his prize Meissen ornaments on the mantelpiece, easy to pick up. I stole down the stairs from his flat calmly. No one would know who I was or where

I came from. A stranger in a foreign land. I had managed the usual trick – meeting him on the top step of an hotel that I was not actually staying in. It works every time.

Computerland

There are those instants when the computer closes down. Shut. Silent. Bang. And all your life is inside it, even if you think most is all squashed inside your mobile. Somehow the computer felt safer –until it wasn't. I had not provided for this. Off to the classified phone book and trying to decode its terse descriptions. Two did not make house-calls.

"We're not like doctors, you know."

"I used to come into people's houses, but not any more." The world expected cars or at least lots of money and I had neither. And that is how I discovered Jem. He arrived at the house with the speed of a fireman. He was tallish, dark-haired, plump and an absolute nerd, but a likeable one. He sat like a concert pianist and confidently rattled the keyboard. He riffled through one item after another without stopping, trawling through several years-worth of items. Mid-afternoon, I made him a cup of tea.

In the gap he told me about how he had been utterly thrilled by computers at school and had left early to work in a call centre.

"Not on the phones, you see, I was maintaining the computers." He relaxed even more. "And thanks to computers, I've just met a girl online, Mai, we communicate every day. My mum says she's not a real girlfriend, just a penfriend, that's all, but we are the very best of friends, very close. Now I'm saving up to visit her." I paid him enough to buy a couple of litres of petrol, enough to get back to where he lived in a village with his parents. Jem left a helpful leaflet full of good simple advice. Six months later, the computer stuttered to another stop. The mouse was not being accepted. Phone up Jem. He waltzed into the house and sat down confidently in front of the blank screen again.

"Notice any difference?" he queried. His black hair *was* a bit longer and glossier and he might have lost about two pounds, but he was still a portly nerd. He waved his left hand. A bright wedding ring. "Well, look at this! Married! I went across to Thailand and we got married. Her family were delighted to meet me. I managed to bring her back, it took a lot of arranging. And she's pregnant! Well, she's one of eleven herself. My friends in the village are all jealous, I've dashed past all they've managed to do in less than a year. And Mai can help me with computer stuff too." All was well in his home then. I think I sent a card to wish them well. People go out of your life and you forget all about them.

And now we move to Christmas, visiting the family, and rushing to get last-minute shopping in town. From watching TV crime dramas, I have a horror of underground carparks. The acres of concrete, the static petrol-filled acid presence of car after car and the sinister echo of voices from afar. Signs saying *EXIT*, far away in the gloom. As my family clustered round the pay machine, a plump man queued after us. Jem. He saw me but did not "see" me. It was so embarrassing that I barged in to break the hiatus and said,

"It's Jem, isn't it? My computer guru!" as I introduced him to my Christmas family. And then I noticed that beside him was an almost unkempt woman, slightly foreign-looking, with a small infant in a push-chair. Asian women have olive skin and glossy blue-black hair. They have delicate lithe limbs. This woman, obviously Mai of the emails, the marriage and the baby, was a world-weary woman of about forty, much older than Jem. Her hair was greasy, an indistinct dark brown and drawn back in a lank ponytail. Her face was more pale grey than olive and the dark Eastern eyes were lack-lustre. There was no gracefulness. An overlarge grey jumper hid her body and the jeans were lumpy, as only second-hand clothes can be. The little boy looked blank, tired, and did not smile up at us at all. They all looked poor and careworn and then I forgot about them in the general Christmas round of relatives and interesting things to eat in so many different houses.

Say it's Easter or thereabouts and the computer went into another decline. I don't know how it happens, I don't go off into games or weird international sites. Perhaps it is micro-chipped to malfunction every six months or so after a certain date. I phoned Jem but there was no answer. Of course, he could have moved out from his parents' address. Tried his mobile in the advert in the classified pages, new edition. Not a recognised number. Of course, he's gone off to Thailand with Mai and the baby. Strange, though, for a computer nerd to disappear like that. What about his business? I tried Google. Perhaps he had a proper office now with its own international number. But there was no trace. Not on the first page of Google. I scrolled on and on, then adding his village and there he appeared. His village's parish news. There he was. Unbelievable. It said he had died suddenly on Boxing Day and as it was such an awkward time, the funeral ceremony would be held over, post New Year. There was even a photo of him drinking with friends.

Emails, marriage, birth, death, funeral; it was like the rhyme of Solomon Grundy. Jem, that cheerful lump of a young man, no longer existed. It was as if he had backed out of a terrible mistake. Perhaps Mai, somewhere back in Thailand (or was it the Philippines?) was carrying on his business? Or was she living with her parents-in-law, contacting customers in their back bedroom while they looked after their grandson?

I still had Jem's instructions for computers. Three years old now, it was already out of date. Three years is a century in computerland. And three years was enough for this computer to close down completely. I went back to the new phone directory and after the usual non-replies and refusals to do house visits, a cheerful man agreed to come round. Trim and whitehaired, George was a retired computer systems controller for a large firm, he implied it was British Telecom or the NHS. He wore a navy business suit. As Jem had been wide, lumpy and affable, George was as narrow as a piece of paper and even more cheerful than Jem. Although he was definitely older, perhaps he was not going to die soon. I ought to have foreseen Jem's death; I get little flashes of foresight now and then, but it had obviously failed in his case

George took over completely, his confidence was infectious and he persuaded me – there was no choice really – that a new modem and security setting was necessary. He marched off with the old machine and reappeared with a shiny black glossy one instead, plus a large bill. He was also wearing a new waistcoat, a neat nineteenth century touch in the circumstances.

Six months or so later – by now I *was* convinced they all put microchips that pinged out precisely at that mark to bring in the consultants once more. George bounced in again, bringing a gale of enthusiasm with him. Like Jem, he did his concert pianist performance, lights changed, screens flashed by and all was well again, time to pay cash on the spot. I did notice his extra bounciness.

"Oh, I'm moving abroad, out of this country, leaving really soon. This country's finished." I had not realised this. The trees, birds, honeysuckle and my weekly pension were all going on as usual. "I won't be here after July. But you can ring me up. I can do it all remotely. Or you can be transferred to Stan in the office supplies shop in town. Yes, I've been across to the Philippines, marvellous place. I can walk down from my office right onto the beach at the end of the day, white sand, surf, sunset." I saw that usual vision of the palm-fringed bar set up on a beach, a couple of people lounging and chatting in the shade, the tide gently lapping the shore. Not at all like Cornwall or Llandudno, my only reference points.

George lived way out in the country, even further away than poor Jem. At least Jem lived in a village; George lived in a huddle of farm labourers' cottages built well before the First World War. I knew nothing of his private life. Wife and children grown up and gone, probably. He phoned up after Christmas, still in England. Something had gone wrong, a delay. Time for my check-up. He bounced in again, this time incongruously sunburnt and full of healthiness. He had changed his previous office-style outfit to jeans, sporty T-shirt and denim jacket.

"Been across again. They love us there. Lovely people. And I did something I've not done since I was twenty or so. Going past a showroom, on the spur of the moment, I went in and bought myself a motorbike. And with the exchange rate it was a fifth of the price. Paid cash too. Wonderful." Sketchy foresight or not, I could see a late, very late midlife crisis going on here. No wonder they loved him – a pale giant going round liberally disposing thousands of pounds cash. And then the last bit of the jigsaw fell into place. I had been stupid not to guess.

"Of course, the traffic's total chaos there, comes in from all sides, it's totally without any rules. And I'm on the bike with nine of us – my girlfriend, her brother, her sister and husband and their two kids in the sidecar and two brothers hanging on somehow." Of course, the little Filipina girlfriend and the happy family so welcoming to the generous man from England. It was Jem all over again, but in a reverse pattern, plus a motorbike. The white rich tech expert, so soon to become a father whether he intended it or not.

Their only link would have been his computer. George, whiling away those empty winter evenings down the deserted country lane, his impatience with the land's slow heart and its watercolour skies.

From Saltash to Castle Carey

In the Second World War, a French Resistance group noted down detailed observations of German troop movements along the train line of the French coast. They pretended to be artists, writers, frequent travellers and so on. This is supposed to be in the same format.

Saltash was not really awake at eight on this February morning. It was like surprising a late sleeper, still undressed. The shopfronts were not on duty yet. The station cat prowled around, efficient and glossy. Beyond the town the fields were quilted in various greens. Borders ramped in all directions like carefully needleworked hems.

Train announcements had told us to contact a member of staff (nowhere about; not seen any of them) or a police officer (ditto.) This was compounded by announcements in Paddington Station at the beginning of the original journey that plain-clothes police were about.

How would you know who was who? And which was which? Either side of the info centre were gigantic screens that showed us who to look for, what a terrorist looked like. Beneath the screens, one of the helpers at the desk looked exactly like the expected villain. Dark skin, black hair, hooked nose, he dispensed train information to all, quite safe, a hero of the movement to diversity.

Turning to the man next to her on the bench, they chatted about the cold, the pigeons, the cancelled trains. Looking at him carefully, his plain face, plain hair and plain clothes, he might have been one of those in disguise, especially as he hurriedly got up and ended their chat without any explanation.

Warning. CCTV in Operation.

Travel was not broadening the mind; it was making it shut up in order to function adequately at all in the midst of so many conflicting realities.

Teignmouth.   Trees like bad hairdos blown about or brushed to one side carelessly.

Red sand chewed up by the waves. Today the waves were delicate, well-behaved and advanced like tiers of lace.

Mist made ordinary towns and cities interesting.

When the mist dispersed their true boring selves reappeared, stubborn and dull hiding behind veils.

A woman in the compartment chatted loudly to an imaginary friend.

Worth every penny.

Bridges' underpasses, their stanchions skirted merrily, like froufrou skirts, with multi-coloured graffiti. It was unreadable from the train, each tag a screaming plea for recognition. We were here; and here. And look at us over here. We don't vote. We just scream our name in protest. Brighter and brighter colours, louder and louder. Silver and gold, silver and useless gold.

Exeter St Davids.   Almost everyone just like London, dressed in black. Only the builders and council workers were in Day-Glo orange. Like prisoners they could never escape, easily picked out in the landscape.

That's the thing.

In contrast almost all travellers were in variations of black as if not wanting to be seen, noticed, picked out. Worse than Mao's China. Don't notice me; or me, I look just like the others. Not brilliant black-velvet black nor even smart navy-blue. Just a general I-am-sad- and shabby black even if it had cost hundreds.

Of course, I understand.

Here and there a small church spire pointed up to heaven. We are all here – are you there, God? For reasons unknown, out here in the countryside the spires were black, which made them look more accusing and bad-tempered, lightning conductors ready for God's thunderous answer. Always silent. No reply.

House alone in a dip, painted yellow, like a dropped bar of butter or expensive soap.

Sheep with black faces like mascara taken to its limits.

If I were you.

Eric Ravillious landscape but more than he could have painted and far more cheerful now that the celebrations (because that's what they really were; propaganda about The Empire) of the First World War were over. The Second World War would have to bide its time, too embarrassing from an EU viewpoint. All friends now.

Clocks on public buildings all telling the wrong time. Said 9.30 when it was 25 minutes past 11 in real life.

It's not intended.

Tiverton Parkway   Copse of trees living their private life. Perhaps they, too, have relationships.

Pools of water in the fields always ruining the centre. Like those model gardens we made as children with the little mirror in the middle of its dried moss lawn and the minute parsley trees. Broccoli, unknown at the time, can be a minute oak tree, if you get it right.

Ah, leaving the weekend free.

Gigantic lorries paralleled the train at times, threading   through lines of black trees. Someone had planted a line of poplars, knowing they would form a glamorous high fence in x years' time, long after the funeral. Now and again a church had only a tower; prayers only half-cooked. Congregation unable to afford the extra finance and finangling that a spire would cost in time and expense. Donor backing down.

I just need to know.

Who are the mystery people who never turn up? Their reservation tickets stand bravely like paper gravestones. Tiverton Parkway to Reading. Truro to London Paddington. Hayle to Plymouth. Penzance to London Paddington; none of them existed. I have their tickets here as proof. What happened to the people? Reserved, Class, coach, direction of travel – all chosen, but no people. Where are they and what are they doing instead?

I'll find that out for you.

Dawlish.　　Caravan site facing a volatile sea and vulnerable to its moods.

Manure left at the side of fields. Eaten, digested and then back to feed more grass unless the cycle is destroyed by interfering humans.

I'll catch up with you tomorrow.

Taunton.　Lines of gigantic yellow engine trucks, Snow ploughs? Looking alien, robot intelligence, alien beings all huddled together waiting for worse weather.

Edges of stations where no one loves the embarrassing land that is neither track nor train nor station. Even buddleia was in retirement on this early February morning. Bicycles stacked together, springy, lithe, all ready to dash off anywhere, like narrow lurcher dogs waiting for their owners.

Flats stacked together. People in different hives but not producing honey.

Corduroy fields. At least they would continue to exist after Brexit as before it. What happened on their surface would be another thing entirely; or several things. It is the top ten inches, oh, the old measurements, that we depend on, the tilth. Green fields streaked with white, as if a lazy artist had dashed off a picture and not come back to finish it. There are boring parts, just fields, hedges and trees. None of them look as if they are doing much now (or ever.) These are the parts that developers have their eye on. Develop, what a wonderful traducement of a word.

At this point the train shook so much that the writing skewed while the fields green-ribbonned along at speed. Snooker-table flat and peaceful.

A trackside scrap-dealers. Discarded cars, people's dreams that came to naught. Thousands and thousands of pounds, car-loans, debts, distances travelled, places, memories. All now merely heaped rusting metal, rather embarrassed, tilted over each other and decaying together. The station's commuters' car park mimics the scrapyard. Still-breathing cars.

The woman has gone silent now, into texting.

Scatterings of discarded snow left in strange corners. Spilt icing sugar at edges of hedges like snow trying to run away and hide. I did not get a Christmas cake this year. (We eat the landscape.) Will cook one for Easter with an extra layer of icing and marzipan in honour of here.

Raggedy farm with outbuildings and assorted debris. You can never get them tidy – too many sheds and equipment and things that must be kept, in case of something different happening. Potential threats bullying the present.

Somerset Levels.   Flooded fields spreading. Moody fields like stale soup.

Moon's surface as builders scoop like moles. Heaps of discarded, dislocated soil littered with trucks, vans, engines, diggers, dumpers and any equipment known to modern humankind. Railside with ghosts of felled trees, chips of trunks scattered. Live wood shavings left as evidence. No leaves on the tracks next autumn.

Perhaps the woman realised I was writing down her every word.

Graffiti on the train signs. Exit, entrance. A housing estate nearby, a busy teenage community. Sir, Madam, do you know where your children go at night? Sudden blue skies over a warehouse.

Cows lying at the sheltering edge of a shed like people entertaining at home. Private.

Sugar-beet factory all on its own with a little concrete carpark surrounded by fields.

Reality cut in two by the train – left side misty like a tonal chart of greys. Right side blue sky and sun in the distance picking out white houses like pearls.

Sewage works. Total mystery no one discusses. Far tidier than some farms, factories or back gardens.

More scatterings of abandoned snow –clues in a detective novel. Snow all along one side of the bank, like that toilet-paper that the puppy drags along in the adverts. And then, is it snow evaporating? White mist rising along a hedge and line of trees.

Then, real snow, more of it behind silhouetted trees. Total white-out. What is the weather forecast? More white mist, nothing is falling though. The trees stand as if nothing was wrong.

There's a waft of perfume as the woman leaves, mixed with the brisk aftershave of a fellow-traveller.

No snow on any roof. Barges like children's wooden toys stranded at side of frozen canals. No sign of life, no smoke from the chimneys.

Sports ground; a white handkerchief, completely square and neatly ironed . A rabbit, quite safe, as no predator is about. The flock of black sheep ignore it.

Snow on some roofs at last, a row of nineteenth century cottages, their attics cladded to within an inch of their life.

A newly-thatched roof. Marzipan, obviously. Straight out of a fairy story. And we are here at last.

Invitations, Sometimes

An invitation, a soirée, a what-have-you, it did not matter. Sonia could sit through any amount of chamber music in a good cause like this, raising money for refugee children. The genteel crowd passed through the hall, showing their gold-edged invitation cards and their passports to prove they were not terrorists, however well-dressed.

Invitations like this do not come often and it would be a chance to have a nose around an entire embassy while looking for the toilets. There were no directions, signs or labels as the embassy was essentially still a private home, though on a grander scale and *olde worlde* style.The décor was what a nineteenth century builder would have knocked together for any industrialist or banker with delusions of grandeur. Dark panelling formed a large reception room which led onto a terrace with sweeping views over wide suburban gardens and the fields beyond.

It was difficult to work out if the house was there because of the view or the view had been kept once these palatial villas had been built, the plasterers and carpenters had shifted their tool-bags and the tired carthorses had trailed the builders' rubble away. next, the gardeners would have arrived and begun to sculpt fashionable gardens. And true to form, the nineteenth century rhododendrons and hydrangeas flourished, leaving no need for modern plants, as they continued to spread gorgeously.

Of course it had not been planned as an embassy. This was obvious from the start. It was as if the ambassador was really an eccentric hiding out here in an old-fashioned villa with a flag hung over the front door. Not even a large flag; more a domestic-sized one. He announced that Madame Ambassador was away for the week. The glamorous young assistant, apparently his only staff, did not look very diplomatic, more like a girl from a secretarial agency.

It was as Sonia walked through the dining room – with its large fourteenish-sized table – and got a glimpse of the kitchen, that she had an idea. Or, to rephrase that, because the English language gives second chances, an idea struck her. Beyond the plain grey modern carpet, no rich Wilton or Axminster whirls of deep reds and royal blues, a door led into a down-market 1970s kitchen. The cabinet doors were Formica, plastic, imitation, cutting edge utilitarian council-house fashion. A bulky old-fashioned cream coloured fridge, looking none too efficient, nestled underneath a shelf crowded with bottles of juices and sauces, condiments and spices jostling against each other. It whirred comfortably to itself.

Beyond the smattering of chandeliers, four exactly, shared between hall, reception room and two in the dining room, here in the kitchen, fluorescent lights blared out every imperfection. Such incessant lighting emphasised each crack and chipped edge and though the place was clean (it must have been,) it looked slummy and sordid.

"My own kitchen's better than that!" Sonia turned to a woman she had met only a minute ago, although they found out they lived near each other. Geraldine agreed.

"Yes, they're all either farmhouse imitation Shaker these days or Ikea's white-ice range."

"Do you know you can buy entire kitchens online these days?"

"We could open our own embassies at this rate. Only need an expandable dining table with extra leaves and you're away!"

"And a flag over the front door."

"Yes, that's a bit of a drag, isn't it. I thought if you were a proper accredited embassy you had to have a proper flagpole, you know, so you could raise the flag and lower it every sunrise and sunset, and you'd have to have it at half-mast when someone important in your nation dies. That's surely one of the main functions of an ambassador like this, hoisting and lowering flags on ceremonial occasions?"

"I could design my own flag. And if I could manage to put up a whirligig clothes dryer in the back garden like I did – you can get a special mix cement delivered, a powder, you know – a flagpole's got to work on the same principle, a post in a cement block. I'll do it. But could you design a flag?" Geraldine said she'd try, as a joke. But looking at Flags of the World in the endpapers of a super-sized geography book in the local library, most designs had already been used. She went for a tie-dye version instead, using half an old single bedsheet. No one could ever copy it. She would have it copyrighted somehow and perhaps make some money by selling postcards of their new flags; because Sonia had to join in the game too. Sonia's flag was purple, with an appliqué rhododendron bang in the centre of it where most flags would have stars or crescents. It was a sign of how impressed she had been by that view from the terrace. It also took a lot of intricate hand-sewing and appliqué work to manufacture it, but once completed, Sonia took a photo to use on a business card, plus some postcards.

Vista Print delivered their new publicity items. Because neither woman was rich or even middling, the expenses came out of their weekly housekeeping and their part-time jobs. Their husbands, Louis and Jim, were amused that their wives, now close friends, were both so happy these days, with repercussions in their marriages.. It was almost as if, now in their forties, a new life had begun, even if different from those first enthusiastic nights of long ago.

Sonia and Geraldine met for tea on Saturday. Neither drank coffee in rebellion against Starbuck's tax evasions; a small mark, even if ineffectual.

"We need a national anthem."

"Each," Geraldine corrected her. "Perhaps we could ask our kids to help with the music? We want to be modern, after all."

"But stately. You have to think of ceremonies and the army having to stand to attention while it's played." Sonia was looking ahead.

"So nothing too merry, then. Perhaps something more classical and slow? That lovely bit from the *Enigma Variations*, I really love that." Sonia persisted –

"But no one would go to war to that, it's too ethereal, too relaxing."

"Well, the English use it in their military melodies, I'm sure I've heard a brass band arrangement of it at Cenotaph Remembrance services."

"My Ben's learning the trumpet."

"But he belongs to *your* embassy, your country. We might even have to go to war against each other one day you know –all countries do, sooner or later." Sonia was set back, nonplussed by this.

"I've just realised, we'll need to invent countries."

"With edges all round."

"And new names." So they chatted in this make-believe world, sitting in the window of Munchie's café, their next week's work list growing. Anthem, music, rousing words, title of country and extent of its boundaries.

"Kilometres or miles?"

"I prefer miles really, though you get less to the pound." Geraldine was the puzzled one this time.

"It's a joke. All sexist too, when men see a well-stacked woman, they say you are getting more to the pound. Or less, in some cases…" Both women were well-endowed with middle-age spread adding more. They were suddenly aware of their appearance. They would have to buy large hats and co-ordinating dress-and-coat outfits in pastel shades. Three-quarter-length gloves might be necessary and low-rise kitten heels for long hours standing at official parades and processions. Their husbands and children would have to be smartened up. Their mundane world was suddenly shot into rainbow colour.

Both Louis and Jim went through the same perplexing experiences where they found their wives rooting through the wardrobe and inspecting their few suits with a speculative eye.

"Well, you might need to have one really good outfit – suit, shirt and shoes in case of anything important cropping up," Sonia said as Jim slouched in crumpled mid-calf chinos, as it was a hot day.

"What's all this fuss about? Has someone died? It's the middle of summer, for Christ's sake." He did not usually swear or blaspheme, but this was a hot day and he was too tired to go mining into his wife's subconscious to get at the real meaning of all this. Jim had learned over the years to keep to the surface; it worked better. Women's minds were a minefield of contradictions, mazes that were badly planned; once you got in there, there was no way out except by a major row. Unlike in the Minotaur, there was no string to guide your escape. So far the two husbands had not met, but their fates were entwined from here on. It progressed merrily on, with perplexed neighbours watching the flags wafting in the wind and Jim or Louis dashing to and fro with their respective lawnmowers crisping up their respective lawns.

Geraldine became the Neighbourhood Watch representative and in competition, Sonia became a School Governor. Their husbands were persuaded into becoming a) a part-time traffic warden and b) a police community support officer. They often met each other, patrolling in opposite directions. Slowly, an uneasy atmosphere arose between them as if they had made a truce or treaty at some time not to interfere in each other's area. Sonia and Geraldine, meanwhile, met less and less in Munchie's, being too busy to concern themselves with wasting time over coffee and cakes.

Their children, sporting little badges and ties in their respective s colours, stopped calling round for each other. Geraldine's children complained about the new school governors' rules and Sonia's children began complaining about being cautioned by Neighbourhood Watch grannies for riding their bikes on the pavement. Bit by bit it degenerated into a quiet hostility as these petty daily quibbles accumulated.

Each family awaited the delivery of its own gigantic ceremonial Christmas tree to place on its immaculate lawn, broadcasting in fairy lights "Peace to All." They sent official Christmas cards to each other. But after a stark winter their two opposing flags flapped limply on their flagpoles, the tie-dye and the appliqué battered by January winds and bleached by February sleet and snow. They communicated solely by email now.

"All decent-sized countries need borders and we never settled that exactly, do you remember?"

"Right. Then you can have from Debenhams to the Town Hall carpark."

"No, I want from Marks and Spencers to the bus station." The silent war had to continue; neither family could back down. Now they were real independent countries and ready for the skirmishes to begin. Both of them had ordered chandeliers from Argos – proper chandeliers with glass pendants – and were eagerly waiting for their delivery.

The Worst Journey Ever

Leo never managed to work out who started the idea of them going on a trip to Marrakech, or even who 'all' started out as. They were coming into their second year at Uni and it was not as if they were studying world development or politics. No, here in Eng Lit it was more to do with the zeitgeist. All the hit parade songs that permeated the airwaves had etched it into their brains. Deconstructing stories had led them to this hybrid of Treasure Island and 'On the Road to Marrakesh.' Crosby, Stills and Nash had a lot to answer for across two continents as students worldwide left for this new destination they had never heard of before.

Graham and Louise, well, they were a couple for starters and then Jim, Andy, Mari and later, surprisingly, Elvira. Perhaps Louise had persuaded her to come along. It wasn't going to be cheap either. Families chipped in some funds; those less lucky did extra shifts in pubs, Tesco's or Sainsbury's.

Graham found a firm that hired out minibuses but Tim, a later addition came in with a second-hand van that had already done the trip there and back. He showed them photos in the students' café and it was enough to cause a mini riot. The van was covered in orange paint with pseudo marigolds and sunflowers swirling over all surfaces except the windows. He volunteered to be the first driver, leading into France.

" A real pioneer, we can take turns after that. It's really cheap," Tim said, "Very cheap. They give us an itinerary and supporting information, it's the next-best thing to having a dedicated driver. We'll save a fortune this way and won't have some superior seen-it-all guy breathing down our necks all the time."

"We do have to cut some corners," Louise jutted in. "We've got enough time, though, to get visas and malaria jabs and apply for passports or see they're all up to date."

Elvira added, "We need insurance, each of us, or all together. There must be some way we could get cover for the trip, for any eventuality."

"Misery guts," Tim replied, "you'd be better spending your money on a good tent and all-purpose sleeping bag. And we need to make up a list of essential stores, like toilet paper for instance." This was too much for the others; this was supposed to be a trip to explore life styles, and for most of them a chance to smoke as much weed as they wanted, once they crossed various borders. The added luxury of enhanced consciousness would be a bonus – they would return enlightened and wide-seeing. Having to make lists of foodstuffs and toiletries was a mundane come-down already. In fact, learning that they would have to do their own cooking on a tiny set-in stove was a real disappointment. It looked like freedom meant either hard work or lots of money for four-star hotels.

A last minute addition was Ben, a former student who still hung around their haunts, a sort of ghost student, fixed in time. He functioned as the university dealer and looked forward to stocking up for the return journey. He was already planning on eyeing up the roof of the van, how to remove a panel and smuggle in a kilo if possible. These innocents would not notice a thing once the trip started.

So the little group assembled at Felixstowe docks, which was the first time most of them saw the brightly–painted minivan, apart from Tim and Andy. They had both hitched down the previous week from Norfolk to see the firm's headquarters, inspect the van and sign various papers.

The actual office was a cluttered table in the corner of a garage along the quayside. Crowding into the Portakabin, the nine of them produced the necessary cash.

"The deposit's paid, you'll all pay the rest of the rental" It was a wrench, parting with so much cash for all of them except Elvira. She came from a rich family and everything was a game to her.

They joined the other cars on the ramp onto the cross-channel ship and after parking on the car-deck, went upstairs to the café. It was here the first shock happened – they did not have any cabins, it had been forgotten in the great plan and none were available now at all. They would have to loll around on the upholstered seats until dawn, semi asleep, as if they had been taken hostages in a café. At least they were first in the queue for breakfasts.

France, of course, drove on the other side of the road and Tim started the day tired and swearing as he adapted to the new regime. Louise wanted to stop off at Paris.

"I prefer France after all, we could stay here instead. I got our school prize for French." Ben was already ashamed of their flagrantly decorated van.

"It's so naïve. We are shrieking out that we're naïve bloody tourists. Should have got a plain old van, make it look as though we roam round the world all the time, or try and look a bit more local, white van man international sort of thing."

They hugged the coastal towns and reached Spain a few days later. The change of temperature affected them all differently. Elvira remained calm and aloof, Tim, Graham and Louise shared some dope,

"We'll get the best red Leb once we get there – we deserve that!" Like his friends, Leo wanted to both boast to his family and also to hide from them the true inspiration for the trip, but he remained an onlooker, not really involved. Spain grew hotter and drier. Jim decided to buy a guitar and said he was inspired by the intense sunlight and the landscape. The others laughed at his attempts. It got more exciting as they crossed the ferry from Gibraltar to Tangiers. They had actually hit Morocco at last.

Mari insisted they go to Casablanca because of the film, but by that time tempers were frayed and it went into the might-do box

"C'm on, we can do it on the way back. It's got a proper airport and all these days, it's not a quaint black and white film stopped in time." Jim objected. Mari wondered if they would manage to get back the same way, they had got lost so often now the entire route was uncertain.

"Tangiers – that's Paul Bowlby and André Gide," Jim giggled.

"Yes, we're going through twentieth century druggies," Elvira sneered. "In fact I'm getting the first plane out of Casablanca, I've had enough already."

She would be recreating the ending of the film, figures on the tarmac, rain on a hot night and 'We'll always have Paris'.

"I thought Buddhist self-enlightenment was what we were after, not a drinking binge," Mari complained.

"Local drink –we don't know what it's made of."

"I can't even read the label, it's in every foreign language except English." All around them sliding signs in Arabic script shut them out from comprehending anything. Language, they were all studying language, and here was the Tower of Babel, with no clues to the code.

Arab boys had broken into the boot and stolen the toolkit while they slept in their various tents.

"People do the darndest things" Ben said. And then he lost it completely, went overboard, berserk, crashing about the tents, screaming and whirling around. Tim threw a precious bucket of water over him, which only made him worse.

"A litre of orange juice and two hours" Louise said, "that's all it takes."

" But that's for LSD," Andy said. "Two more hours of this and we'll have no camp left."

"It's better than nothing, just sitting round and pretending," she replied.

In the morning, they found that Andy's new Spanish girlfriend, a girl he had met in a café, had run off with his wallet and Jim's new guitar. After that they all had to swear on the map that no new lovers, however attractive, would be accepted in their group of nine. Being free spirits did not mean they could give everything away to strangers.

Mosquitoes were eager to get fresh pale blood and they were soon a mass of bites. Leo had it worst and had to go to a small hospital, where the language barrier did not matter, the inflamed bites showed his problem vividly.

Leo lay in the makeshift bed, he could hear the slow clang of the now-and-again air conditioner. Thinking it over, it had been enlightening, but he could not say how exactly. He was in a hospital somewhere, he had been in a fever and now he was in a befogged state where he had no cares.

Ben landed up in prison – they promised him every bit of help, but their money and visas were running out, so they had to leave him here in the British Consul's hands.

Like a minuet or gavotte in any Jane Austen novel, the couples had changed partners. No more Graham and Louise. The settled normality of long-term couples was gone; the atmosphere now was rife with high-octane sexual tension. No one was safe, like chess pieces they were moved around, constantly unsettled.

"Travel chess games," Leo muttered to himself. "Chess games." Dope smoking of the highest calibre had only added to the mix. The happy band of travellers had turned into a mixture inside a fermenting jar.

The outcomes could not have been foreseen, as some puzzled parents received their disillusioned children back home over a month later. The cheery Marrakesh song emphasised how the innocents had been duped, and it stubbornly remained in the charts for months afterwards, mocking their dreams of running away to a new and better world.

Park Bench

It was going to be a lucky day after all. Mrs Grossman said would Emma take the two children out to the park this afternoon, just forget about all the cleaning. It would save an afternoon of dusting, away from the minefield of Dresden shepherdesses with their abundance of shredded coconut-like texture that collected dirt magnificently. She wondered how Mrs Grossman had collected such monstrosities and decided they were from the husband's side and probably forced mementoes that Mrs Grossman, for all her modern ideas, could not get rid of now. Noblesse Oblige, even across mantelpieces.

The afternoon appointments did not always get the best out of the workers, sent out by the agency to different houses each day. This morning's job had been gruelling, taking bin after bin of rubbish down several flights of stairs as the Feldman's kitchen in Abercromby Mansions was going to be decorated next week. Emma had cleaned the kitchen cupboards and washed the walls so well that Mrs Feldman had said it almost did not need painting at all.

Today was becoming sunnier as well; so much nicer to be off in the park than hoovering round an already clean flat or coping with a mound of ironing. She was also relieved about being saved from ironing, a useless chore of worshipping cloth and giving it a transitory perfection that it did not need. It just chewed up energy. She had no experience in ironing shirts at all, as at home her father's shirts were always sent to the laundry, but that was no excuse in the here-and-now. Last week the iron had slipped off the edge of the ironing board and had fallen onto the floor but she had not summoned up enough courage yet to tell Mrs Grossman about it.

After loading the pram with a bottle of rose-hip syrup and various cloths and toys nestling round the baby Anne, Emma took little Tom downstairs. He was a cheerful youngster and was already at nursery school a couple of days a week.

"Now, hold onto the pram and stay right beside Emma," Mrs Grossman told him. Then,turning to Emma, "Take your time, and we'll have tea early when you get back." She was Swiss and was markedly different from all the other employers, with a surprisingly democratic point of view. One afternoon she had a woman friend visiting, and the friend was visibly discomforted that Mrs Grossman had Emma sitting there at the table with them and having tea and cakes with them like another guest. The woman could barely speak to her normally and was obviously embarrassed.

"We treat everyone as far as possible the same, and our country has referendums to decide policy. We all vote," Mrs Grossman said. "I am proud to be a Swiss. I have kept a dual nationality on my passport."

The park was nearby, not too far for Tom's little legs. It was something left in its Victorian state, no council modernising had ruined its layout, the prim flowerbeds and curved pathways were like something from a sepia postcard. Here and there old people were sitting on weathered benches, probably part of their daily routine. An old man smiled at her as they walked past, then went back to reading his Daily Mail. Tom had been given a bag of breadcrumbs and they soon had a mass of sparrows darting about, fighting merrily for the fragments. Tom was delighted at this little kingdom of birds at his feet and not so happy when, frightened by a dog, they all flew away.

They rounded the pathway past clumps of rhododendrons that blocked out the light with their invasive leaves creating gloomy caves. It was deserted here with overgrown greenery. A man appeared suddenly, as though he had been standing within one of the huddle of bushes and had chosen this moment to emerge into the sunlight.

"Excuse me, do you have a moment?" Emma was puzzled why he needed to know. He came nearer, giving a glance on either side. "I'm an undercover policeman. There have been a couple of attacks on women in this area and we are holding a crime reconstruction this afternoon. Would you just stand still here in this corner, by these branches, so we can have some idea of how the probable situation would have been?" He had the usual detective's mac, exactly the same style as Columbo, but it was darker and longer, unusual on such a hot afternoon. "My colleague will be taking some photos." He looked back over his shoulder into the dark clustered rhododendron leaves. There was too little light to see whether anyone was there, but there was the impression, a feeling of an extra presence in the gloom, someone else waiting.

Emma had been brought up to trust the ' if you want to know the time, ask a policeman' type of officer from the Dixon of Dock Green days. It was her duty to society to help here.

"But I 'm looking after these children - I can't go and leave them on their own out here on the path," she objected. You did not answer back to a policeman. He looked at the pram and dismissed it as not important. Children were obviously irrelevant in these circumstances. This was for adults only. Tom was not looking at him, busy with the chattering sparrows which had returned and followed him for further crumbs.

"It won't take long. You'd be helping the police in an investigation," he said. It was important, exciting, like something on TV. She was wondering what to do, what was best, it was expected of her to help the police, when she noticed he was chewing gum. A stark instant of change. However modern the police were getting these days, with whatever new methods of crime prevention, loitering in parks wearing long macs on a hot summer day and chewing gum would not be one of them. Fear and realisation hit her at once. Luckily she had not let go of the pram handle and Tom was on the other side of the path where he could still see the few sparrows who had returned to the remains of their crumbs. Emma looked into the man's dark eyes and saw something different now, sly.

"I certainly won't be doing anything like that. You must think I'm stupid!" She saw him falter in a way no real policeman would do. He drew back into the rhododendrons as if he wanted to hide and Emma moved away down the path, back to where the benches were, although who could she tell about this? The unidentified man was perhaps already disappearing out the other side.

Now it was over, she felt more frightened than while it was actually happening.

Emma wanted to tell the old man reading the newspaper what had happened but he had already gone, and the bench was empty. She needed his plain reassurance, his everyday ordinariness, newspaper and all. There was no one about. The park was deserted in the sultry afternoon. Paths led off in all directions. Overgrown bushes screened the view and there was a sultry smell from the blossoming and neglected privet. If anything had happened, no one would have heard her screaming. It was scary. She sat on the bench to think things over and calm down. Thank goodness Tom would not be able to tell his mother how near to danger they had been. She moved off to the children's playground where at least there was some company and the cheerful chatter of youngsters on the swings and climbing frames. It was Tom's afternoon out, after all.

Perhaps she should phone up the police – there was a phone-box somewhere along one of the side roads. Had she really seen one, or was it her imagination? But Tom would wonder what she was saying. The police would have to come round to Mr and Mrs Grossman's and interview her. Perhaps she should tell Mrs Grossman? She was a liberally-minded person after all. There would be a lot of fuss. But somehow Emma felt she was to blame for the entire episode herself and that the only result would be no more trips to the park. They strolled back to the flat along the leafy roads, semi-detached houses all so deceptively respectable and boringly safe.

In the wide hallway Emma lifted a sleepy baby

Anne out of the pram and encouraged Tom up the two flights of stairs to the flat and sat down to Mrs Grossman's tea and cakes, wondering if she had imagined it all. These were things you did not talk about as somehow all the shame was left deposited on herself, like the dirt she daily cleaned from other people's houses. Forever she could still see the darkness of the massed rhododendrons, the pit of dark evergreens with their massed candelabras of red blossoms.

It was a week or so later that the papers were full of an account of a young woman seriously assaulted in the nearby park. Emma could see the thick blossom-laden bushes of the rhododendrons, their prim Victorian lushness and the waiting trap behind them. It might be too late now to go to the police, but she would have to make a real decision soon.

Mozart Effect

Sunday afternoon, their favourite time, and Mozart's Piano Concerto No 17 spinning out across the room; Liz thought there could be no greater contentment than this. She sat on the carpet, leaning against Mal, who was listening with his eyes closed, lost in the music.

"Do you know the demand for classical music goes up in wartime? People need the security and its calming effect, and Mozart is the best for stress relief." Mal sat back on the couch, at peace with the world. Liz remembered that comment when their relationship frazzled to a stop soon after and Mal abruptly announced that he was moving out. He must have been in a strange state at the time. It was the usual excuse, it was him needing a change, and it wasn't anything to do with her. Good friends and all that, the usual twaddle. He just needed this break to sort himself out.

But bit by bit the truth came out about what was really going on. He had to admit it eventually, when he came back to collect any letters that had arrived for him. Bit by bit it came out that Mal had moved into a shared house in Shoreditch and there was, surprisingly, Carrie, a new girlfriend he had met at work. He was gone by the end of January and had taken all his belongings including his music collection of CDs, tapes, old records and his guitar. The empty shelves in the living room showed up how much his interests had filled up the space. Liz spread her books out, trying to fill the gaps. But nothing could change the atmosphere in the flat. She wandered around the three rooms listlessly. There was also all that extra rent to pay now.

In Shoreditch Mal hurried home through the February snow, in a rush hour that was as much torture for drivers as the stragglers walking along from the bus stop. He was too vain to wear a cap and he regretted it now. The pavements were slushy and his shoes squelched as he walked up the path, stamping the sleet off in the porch. The upstairs light was on, that meant Carrie was already home. He looked forward to the chance of them both sitting by the warm fireside downstairs and a life-saving cup of tea before the others in the shared house got back from work. But first Mal had to hide the precious box of handmade Belgian chocolates bought for St Valentine's Day early next week.

"Just got to get out of all these wet clothes," he called to her and after shaking his coat and slipping off his shoes, he dashed upstairs and hid the chocolates in his side of the wardrobe in their own room.

"Right. Don't be too long, the tea's made already and it's Swiss roll again!" Carrie worked as a waitress at Moore's Hotel and could sometimes bring left-over cakes home for an extra treat on days like this.

Tuesday dawned with much better weather and a Valentine card each. At breakfast they exchanged gifts – a navy and grey tie for Mal, with a CD of Mozart; Carrie knew it was his favourite.

Mal had chosen a cheap silver bracelet and a single red rose with the box of chocolates for Carrie. Impulsive as ever, she opened it right away.

"Don't worry! It's OK! I'm not going to eat one of them right now, we've just had toast and marmalade! We'll wait until tonight, with something good on TV, we can tuck in then." But then her expression changed.

"What's the matter?" Mal was puzzled.

"There's blue mould on these, like little patches of fog! Look!" Carrie showed him the mottled chocolates in their glamorous box.

"That's got to be from damp. There's been water on them" He knew it was not from last week's bad weather, he had carefully kept the parcel, well wrapped, inside his coat, guarded against the snow. It had to be returned and he dreaded a lot of fuss at the shop, causing bad feelings all round, a credit note or a replacement or something else. But it was not as bad as Mal expected, the shopkeeper was calm and proficient, and dealt with it easily.

"You would have been OK, though, they are not poisonous," he joked, "But, yes, it does look rather strange." Mal's present was not perfect either; he had preferred Vivaldi for some time now, but had not mentioned it to Carrie, who was not interested in any classical music whatever. Everyone had a blank spot and this was hers.

"We have enough noise, living in a city, without adding any more. Our brains are too busy these days filtering out sound, I read it in the papers," she said. "I'd like to live in the country, with just natural sounds like birdsong, even crows and cockerels, I wouldn't mind that at all."

Almost break time in the sweet factory. Today Liz had been moved over from the marzipan department to the chocolate department. A long line of women stood at a conveyor belt, placing specific chocolates into the small boxes. She was put to supplying strawberry centred ones, while other women dealt out hazelnut, coffee crème, truffle and others. They were so expensive that only eight sweets were in each box. The well-designed gold-covered boxes sped past as the women tried to keep up. Intercoms played music continuously across the entire factory, to keep up the workers' spirits. Occasionally the women sang along to a pop song they all knew.

At one part of the factory between the three departments, it was possible to stand and hear all three different sounds at once, in a pop-soup of chaos. Beyoncé belted out against Abba and Coldplay. Past and present mixed together, bringing up different responses. The older women reminisced to the Supremes and Elvis; the younger ones liked Ed Sheeran and Ariana Grande. Sometimes they complained that it was giving them headaches but the sound was never switched off.

And then, startlingly, the tannoy was playing a piece by Mozart. Mozart was definitely no rock star but this piece of his music had recently become popular, since it was used in a TV advert, everyone heard it almost every day now. The incongruous Eine Kleine Nachtmusik played out across this entire factory department. Liz, startled, began to cry. It was 'their tune' when Mal and herself were a couple, and moving into their first flat together in Wood Green. She could not stop herself.

Tears rained down, landing onto the clutches of chocolates as they sped past. There was nothing she could do. Angie, working opposite her, dealing out the truffles, stared sympathetically as Liz searched for a handkerchief.

"Welcome to the Sadness Factory," Angie joked. More boxes sailed past, as Liz threw in the usual strawberry whirls, hardly able to see through tear-filled eyes. Mal and herself, sitting listening to Mozart, going to concerts, avid for more music, and planning on which of the Proms at the Albert Hall they would go to that summer, all that had gone forever. She had never quite understood his fascination with classical music, but had been totally drawn along with his enthusiasm.

And now, here was the messy break-up to cope with as Mal drifted off to move in with Carrie, leaving Liz to keep up their old flat. She had to work extra shifts now to manage paying his share of the rent. Soon she would have to flat-share somehow, turn the living room into a bed-sit to make up the difference or move away to any cheaper place that was within reach of work.

The dancing elegance of Mozart soared over the shift workers, busy stacking more and more boxes of hand-made exclusive chocolates for St Valentine's Day. Some of them looked up as the unusual piece of music swirled round them and one of the women explained it was on TV, that travel advert, had they never seen it?

But after their morning tea-break the foreman was waiting for them when they got back from the staff canteen. He was speeding up the conveyor belt right now, he said.

"You all see this here?" He pointed to the pallets nearby. "Well, we've got to get all this stack filled up by tonight!" the foreman told them. "The night shift can't do it all – you've got to pull your socks up and reach the target. No slacking! You won't even be catching up with Christmas at this rate!"

Off the boxes would go, into storage, lorries, distributors, supermarkets and corner shops. St Valentine's Day was important. All sorts of relationships would blossom, their romance helped along by music, chocolates and red roses. Meanwhile the chocolates waited in the near-frozen warehouse which was totally silent, away from any trace of the sparkling music. The pleasure they would give was locked away in the icy silence.

Thursday night was late-night shopping, luckily, so on the way home, Liz dropped into W.H.Smiths to see if they had a CD of The Best of Mozart. Eine Kleine Nachtmusik was now settled at number one in the charts, amazingly, all the way from 1787 to this rainy evening in Tuffnell Park. Taking it home was regaining part of her past and making it new. It would not be a way of grieving, it would be a fresh start. She could buy a bunch of flowers from the stall outside the tube station too, it would make the evening complete, and brighten up the flat. At least she could afford this small luxury for the time being. And she could get a book from the library to read up about the life of Mozart as well, it had always been a mystery how he managed to produce so much in such a short life.

Next week she would start looking for a new job. Everything was going to change now. She could make her own collection of music, beginning with Rimsky Korsakov's *Scheherazade*, fascinated with the excerpt that was being played right now in the shop. Wild colours swooped around, she had never experienced anything like this before. Its swirling drama was enough to open a new world. Definitely, she would buy it as soon as she was paid tomorrow.

Enemy of the State

The television licence people sent their annual threatening letter. Someone was going to come round and she would end up in prison. Going to the Post Office to assure them there was no TV in the house no longer worked. The man behind the counter was surprised.

"We don't issue licences any more. You do it online or perhaps by telephone. It's all changed. You'll have to buy a computer soon to be able to tell them that you haven't got a television." Then relenting after his flat joke, he added, "There's half hours on computers available up at the library, it's open four days a week, still, I think," and he went back to the next customer.

The electricity company came round to have a look at the meter, to see if it was really registering the correct amount of electricity being used. The meter man looked at it disapprovingly, then looked at her disapprovingly, then he placed an official seal on it, the sort suitable for buried treasure or a crime scene.

"You are not using the usual amount of electricity," he accused.

"I don't have a mower or hedge-strimmer and indoors, I don't hoover or iron," she said unhelpfully. No reaction. "And there's no microwave, food processor or dishwasher."

"How do you know your dishes are bacteria free? Dishwashers are important these days," he defended his electric kingdom. He pasted a large red-printed label over the meter, stating the perils of interfering with the electricity supply. With a last sad disapproving look, he left.

The gas company also sent a man round (was she on a list somewhere?) in shirtsleeves, short combat trousers and hiking boots. He stood there without any identity card, most unprofessional. The emblazoned van was his calling-card. It did not matter. You could get identity cards laminated at any print shop and pretend to be anyone these days. No-one knew how to check and you were supposed to ring head office if anything was suspicious, leaving the pseudo-caller outside, very embarrassing all round, especially if the conversation had to be done through a letterbox.

He tinkered round with pipes and sealants and also put a label on his meter. More cheerful, he accepted a cup of tea and strode off, dressed as a rambler. She wondered if head office knew about this new dress code.

She discovered that the new rubbish bins were issued with pay-by-weight calculators cunningly hidden under the lid. A leaflet came through the door. It stated that people who did not produce the expected amount of rubbish would be investigated. It stressed the social cost of illegal dumping and the threat to the countryside…it wittered on in officialese. They had special helicopters on duty to check down country lanes for any infringements, checking for traces of smoke rising.

Anyone starting a bonfire would be investigated. It all provided employment. Every action was being monitored now.

The sewage company sent a refund of £9, which was really noble of them. At least they could not accuse her of excreting elsewhere, although it was noticeable that the number of public toilets was decreasing rapidly across cities. No one had protested about this covert change in city life.

The water company hedged its bets by post. There was a £25 overpayment so far. They would be sending someone round to test the water meter, she supposed, plus give a veiled look at her personal hygiene and state of clothing and send in a report.

A knock at the door. A representative from a hairdresser's was calling house to house, trying to drum up trade. The sprite-like black-haired young man had a strict fringe, to demonstrate his skills. He stood there being charming and asking how often she visited hairdressers.

"I cut my own hair."

"May I see?" She turned round while the hairdresser stood shocked. "It's not too bad, but you do really need professional styling, not merely a repeat of cutting the ends off." He was not pleased.

"I can't afford people like you, sorry. Soon we'll be filling our own teeth as well. It's what they call small-purse landscape round here." And with that, she shut the door.

A man from the council, something to do with community policing, called the next week.

"Are we supposed to police ourselves now, to save money?" she asked.

"Not exactly, but if the public's involved, obviously that frees up the real officers. Perhaps you would like to join a local group?" She said that, having no television and buying no newspapers, she knew nothing about the local crime rate.

"What on earth do you do with all that spare time, then?" he looked at her, demanding to know.

"*What on earth*...now, that's a very good thought! Yes, I'll join. All right, where do I sign?"

And that was how it all started.

The phone rang one sunny afternoon. A posh voice. Number withheld, always a sign of trouble. She expected the worst.

"You probably don't know about this department yet, it has been set up only recently. We are charged with representing a new government think-tank. We are deeply interested in people like yourself. In these energy-competitive times, there is a need to deliver a new kind of household signalling the move into a post-energy age. You seem to fit that profile according to general utilities' records which we have been researching." He went on and on. Now she was a 'gatekeeper' who could 'deliver' to the new society they were just inventing. The first meeting of the local community monitoring group had not even got round to its first meeting. This sounded more interesting, plus a few more bars up the scale.

Temped to say no, she thought, it's time. Time that the hippies were proved right. It's our revenge. The punks had been sent in, invented as a chaser, to clear all the landscape from all that socialist community stuff and making your own clothes. No profit-margins for outsiders to grab. Too much of that sharing and low-level consuming. Apart from the dope, that worm in their Eden apple, but no society is perfect. The voice glided on almost hypnotically. They probably had lessons in how to do this.

"The revolution has changed how things are run. Unless things are profoundly modified all countries are going to have a bumpy ride. We need some really radical thinkers. You are one of the few ones left. So many have died already."

"Well, I'm used to being disapproved of."

"Far from it. We've been tracking you for some time, for comparison. You've come out top in the low-usage category in your area. We can foresee your next year's consumption pattern and we want other households to replicate it. Your way of life is valuable."

By the next week she was part of a government think-tank, refusing the showers of money they offered.

Although she wanted to go by bus and train and tube, a car was dispatched to collect her from the nearest railway station.

"Government policy" was all the chauffeur would say. He rebuffed any attempts at conversation, which was probably government policy as well. Power was given to her, unasked. Sitting at an official table with other policy-makers, she was asked for ideas and started off helter-skelter.

"Whoever your previous advisers were, those people are downright silly. Once, they were urging us to buy, consume, waste, throw away and buy bigger next time and use up quicker. Now there's less advertising needed, so, street advert hoardings should be pulled down, neon advertising signs can be dismantled, less shop-to-drop activity and posh people forced to use buses. It's going to be complete reversal. These new laws have moral values."

"For a start, I will institute a plant inspectorate to come round gardens and homes, to inspect any plant cruelty. Anyone paving, tarring, cementing or decking will be fined or imprisoned or both. Anyone living on a bus route will be forbidden to either own a car or park on any road included on bus routes."

Frantic activity began all over the country. For a while most streets, especially in suburban areas, were like building sites. Skips hampered passing traffic as garden after garden was dismantled with blocking and terrazza-ing ripped up and parched soil re-exposed to the air. Worms were almost jumping for joy as decking and paving were taken away and real earth reappeared. Sales of spades rocketed and garden centres had to recruit extra staff. Books on gardening sold out, library shelves on 'gardening' category emptied and allotment-keepers, savvy old men and women, were hunted down and plagued for advice and examples.

In a reversal of their usual importance, city centre residents hot-footed it to anywhere countrified for help. Local village halls arranged meetings, parish councils and parish magazines gave encouraging advice. Journalists pounced on all this activity, taking it as the latest news, having trouble with Latin spellings and correct plant names. Cuttings, seedlings, seeds and even prunings were swapped or stolen.

People re-learnt how to make and mend at home, from carpentry to cheese-making. Small workshops erupted in lockups and garden sheds. The sales of hammers and saws and sewing machines went up. There were sounds of men whistling as they got down to work. The crisis in masculinity faded away. There was so much that had to be done now, old skills rediscovered.

In Wales, the midlands and the north, what was left of car manufacture was reined in and a new scheme of production was initiated.

"It's like the war, see, not a time for shrinking violets. We've got to produce buses and coaches now, by the ton-load. No more luxury cars for just one person to swan about in. Less cars than ever." Managers could see the benefit in this and subcontractors, especially those involved in upholstery were cock-a-hoop with visions of future profits. There were more seats needed in buses and coaches than in any motors.

"Tell anyone who objects that blacksmiths and tanners and lace-makers all had to go through the same process in the past. Some trades had to diminish. No manufacturer or union, either side of the political divide has a right to continue forever." Memories of the wounds inflicted by Thatcherdom were still raw, especially in the north; but this time it was said to be for their own benefit, not just for the profit of distant shareholders.

As a sweetener, however, and a bright green idea, carthorses were put into an intensive breeding programme. As they existed on grass, oats and food-scraps there was no oil involved and they produced manure at the other end. At last there was a point to all those apparently unused, unnecessary fields and this became a viable objection to encroaching on greenfield sites by marauding developments. Petrol-free carthorses munched away at the greenery and made little noise.

The country was hurtling merrily along, but outsiders were disapproving. International monetary elites could see that they were getting edited out of an entire culture. Money was being passed around slowly, with far less opportunities for middlemen to grab a piece of the action. It looked like the ordinary people were getting more of the economy into their own grasp, for a change. Bartering was thriving and beginning to ruin the Gross National Product, as it was unmeasurable and could not be taxed.

No traceable money equalled no tax gathering, which equalled no fun for government (a group of people in a room, she knew.) Whatever tax was brought in was spent right away on policing and defence. Far worse, there was not much left after for posh expenses like the Royal Family or the friendly grey pockets of corruption.

She was brought in for a private interview at Government headquarters. The tweed-jacketed man looked suitably sad.

"We are sorry about this but it has to be done right now, as soon as possible. We have been censured by the international business community, America especially and other interested parties – the EU is absolutely jumping up and down. We have had to apologise unreservedly for the mistakes made throughout this plan. Matters will have to change to regenerate the fiscal health of the nation. This department is being disbanded forthwith."

They explained that she would be placed in a comfortable, even luxurious, secure unit, a secret prison hotel that was reserved for high-flown embarrassing cases.

"Don't worry, it's all symbolic, you'll be out in a certain time, it's all about saving face internationally. We are having to rein in our policies in response to – er-objections outside our jurisdiction and the threat of sanctions. We are calling it clerical errors and other fudges. You'll be kept there in comfort of course. Just long enough to let the furore die down.

"And how long will that be?"

"I have no idea."

Grounded

As he stood waving down the green and white planes there was an almost tender relationship between the groundsman and the machines. Arms either side, he gestured down, down, repeatedly until the plane nosed to within a few yards of him. When the bond of trust was complete, the plane almost eating out of his hand, he would cross both fists above his head. It was both a gesture of triumph and surrender.

Between the metal and the glass, the pilot and himself had combined, like two men helping a wild animal which did not trust either of them. It was more poignant in the rain, when the groundsman merely turned aside at the instant of the landing-stop and went off in the splashing downpour to a van, or off to do something humble until he was needed, his dayglo jacket becoming dim in the darkening distance.

Whoever the man was, whoever's duty it was, each one of them became beautiful. She watched them while pretending to dust the potted plants scattered round the airport buildings. As these were all plastic, no gardening firm had a contract to maintain or minister to them. Automatic plants, they needed no water nor did they grow extra leaves or shoots. No roots started to creep out of the bottom of the pots. She began to collect cloths and dampened them with water from the Ladies,' going round and brightening up the displays of plants, making the dusty green leaves shiny again, mimicking nature.

Him and his fake birds outside and me and my fake nursery in here. One of the men smiled at her once, but she frowned and moved a large imitation parlour palm so that their eyes could not meet again. A cold November afternoon – holidaymakers from Spain trooping through, flipping their sandals and being ramshackle with happy displacement.

She hoped he had a nice home to go to, a fire burning, just like the adverts, perhaps. A wife who might be harassed, preoccupied, but who loved him enough and who had time enough to have a good dinner ready for him, the front door opening and the smell of a roast or a casserole or the borage gas of Spaghetti Bolognese. Not that she wished for a *hausfrau* fate for any woman; but only cooking could warm a house and revive a man after a day like this of rain driven across concrete and his duties to the metal giants, their moves and swerves. Little vans, with their white and green logos shot past, removing puddles into other puddles.

Unlike in American war films, the groundsman had no table-tennis bats to signal with, just his bare hands. it was that. It made it sexy, the bare hands, that gesture of submission before the planes.

Some days she blended in with the passengers and sat chatting, giving directions to the best taxi rank, where to get a bus and where the B&B district was. She got invitations to stay all over the world, people gave their addresses freely and she made some vague promise to follow them up. But she had no mobile. At first it was their own cards or pages torn out of their diaries but this accumulated so much rubbish-bits that she bought a small notebook from the stationery shop to keep them in alphabetical order. Then someone left their Filofax on one of the telephones and as it did not have very much in it – a person with few friends or who knew all their addresses by heart, she had no problem with taking it over and using it. Prudently, she had also kept the currency notes and travellers cheques.

Out in the downpour, one of the men was placing chocks in front and behind the wheels. Small blocks, but important. Then he wheeled the blue stairs across to the plane door, which opened.. His partner dashed across for that final push, while he locked it under the wheel. An air hostess darted down the steps from the plane, wearing a dayglo jacket too, pointing the passengers over to the right entrances back at the airport. The passengers had to be protected from their own baggage-van which careered across their straggling line. One bag dropped off into the rain. Chevron Texaco tankers and Shell Oil vans zoomed carelessly around.

She managed to keep decent using the Ladies.' The handwash liquid worked as a shampoo and hair was easily dried under the hand-drier, though it was noisy. When she had gone with Ben on a demo to Brussels, that was how they had spruced themselves up. Laughing, she had danced round the departure lounge,

"Look! Quite clean and glossy, even if it's against the rules." But Ben had looked serious.

"They haven't made those rules up yet. It's people like you that make nations fascist. You keep doing what the authorities haven't thought of yet. Then they have to manufacture even more detailed rules, to pin us all down, all because of you and your inventiveness."

The baggage man had to take each item by hand and heft it on to an open truck. All the luggage came out of the plane's side from a conveyor belt, like blood issuing from a wound. (Some planes, though, she could see the hands of the handler, throwing, sorting, shoving it out from the hatch set in the ribs of the plane's body.) The air hostess minced down the set of stairs at the back of the plane with a full black bin-liner, like a housewife putting out the rubbish. First passengers were already approaching, walking past a dayglo man with a clipboard.

The previous luggage had only just been taken off; now the conveyor belt was switched onto reverse and the new collection of suitcases lumbered into the plane's further belly. Spare empty baggage trailers zoomed around, toy cars into splashing distance.

Bottles of water were left everywhere. Sweets were dropped, and coins. The cafés had sell-by sandwiches to throw out; she had discovered the backdoors and entries which had "Staff Only" on them. A purloined all-surface cleaner in its plastic syphon and some Jeye-cloths (top of cupboard, lower departures floor, Ladies) gave her anonymous entry through these doors. Bits and pieces accumulated. A worker's identity label left by a window seat gave her access to roam all over the airport buildings.

Clothes were a problem at first. She strayed into the baggage reclaim area and removed a large suitcase from Russia, the passengers having landed over two hours before. It had been left circling round and round the carousel, a discarded life. A man's, unfortunately, but she removed the toiletries bag, tried the jeans and jumper on and put the rest back. Each day now she inspected the unclaimed pieces, returning each one after removing underclothes, perfumes, shoes and good towels. Washing these was no problem; a collection was built up of serviceable clothes and any dirty ones got returned to lost luggage in their turn.

There were small dramas to witness. She sat and watched while two middle-aged men dressed in beige were being coaxed by a young attendant in shirtsleeves.

"You have to have your baggage weighed first." They looked reluctant, hugging their foreignness to them. He led them to the check-in counter ahead of the other passengers. A man in a black suit appeared from behind a screen and both he and the shirt-sleeved attendant shooed the transaction through. For reasons unclear from where she sat, they walked away from the check-in desk, still with their baggage. A long silver snake of linked trolleys went past with its own attendant guiding its jittery wheels, and the two men were hidden back in the crowd again. It was all half-stories, bits of sense, only the middles exposed.

A shaft of sunlight turned a lone man into a Michaelangelo sculpture, surrounded with a tableau of mixed suitcases. She had forgotten why she was here, what had started this. There had been the excitement of seeing someone off. (Who? Was it important any more?) Then there had been the big questions raining down on her, the lager whys and she had gone into the airport chapel, down an almost secret alleyway. They had moved it to a new place; this was the old one, left over, forgotten. It had an embroidered prayer-mat on the floor, as now it was a multi-faith sanctuary. She had stayed and prayed and cried until what must have been night and then had rolled out the prayer-mat to take away the cold of the tiles. Then she had just stayed, unnoticed, afraid of going back into the outside world again, safe in this airside cocoon.

The groundsmen wore thick, almost mediaeval boots and dark trousers that were the colour of tarmacadam, a weathered near-grey black. There were many doors that opened at a touch; no traveller, worrying about getting to Aghara or Mahon would be going round trying doors here and there. At night these were not locked; she acquired stray shoes, combs, an empty handbag, bits of make-up left by the counter staff of various airlines. Habituated to casual pilfering, in fact doing it so well that it became a skill, she purloined someone's passport. A travel-sick woman was traipsing from toilet to washbasin, throwing water on her face and gulping it down from the taps marked' This is not drinking water.' A passport gleamed out its golden design from the outer pocket of her handbag as the woman dashed back to vomit yet again in the toilet.

Looking idly at the photograph, an image of herself gazed back. They were similar in face and age, herself and this traveller. in an instant she decided, removing the boarding pass too. Some travellers' cheques fell out. It was so easy.

A mild wind scattered a lone piece of paper across the concrete as the straggling group of passengers crossed towards the waiting plane. Standing regally, wearing a blue cape, a blonde air hostess clutched a clipboard, smiling dutifully as each person passed by. The last of the luggage was being shunted into the belly of the aircraft. Finished with that task, one of the groundsmen walked towards her with an open-air confident walk, his eyes searching her face, ready to smile, as if he knew her.

Writer's Details

My stories and books would be described as literary, although that can sound pretentious. It means good old-fashioned plain writing, like the cooking in our childhood.

In Art School, painting was not enough for expressing all the ideas chasing round, and I had always written poems and then short stories too. A couple of discarded would-be novels date from that time and I might resurrect them now, they are almost history.

There's no routine at all. I'd say it was more to do with phases of the moon (joke.) Nothing for weeks or months and then total dedication all day and evening. My writing space is a gigantic desk set in the living room. It is the kind of desk from old black & white films, the solicitor's office or the Head of Police. It's strange to be sitting this side of it. I won second place in Poetry Pulse and the prize-money paid for most of it.

I never call myself a writer, as it is such an easy occupation to claim. For most writers it is not a 9 to 5 five days having to clock in each weekday with only two weeks and official days off a year. Many writers use the label as a way to social climb and claim grants and allowances. If pushed, I'd say I was an artist.

Research is fatal! It's like going off on a short walk and ending up miles away, happily lost. It just entices you to unearth more and more, absolutely fascinating details - and then you have totally useless pages and pages of notes and printouts. And then you don't like to throw them away.

Editing – I write by hand on A4 pads, 160 pages, narrow lines. Then off to the computer and type, sifting through the lot. Then print off all the pages, make a pot of tea (well, several,) and then, with a red pencil, go through each line. I went to a grammar school and we learnt to parse, going through 'Parts of Speech,' which does not happen these days. Each word has its dedicated function. There are only eight categories: noun, verb, pronoun, adjective, adverb, preposition, conjunction and exclamation.

There is a fashionable movement against using adverbs and I even read in one magazine's requirements that adjectives should be as sparse as possible. That will lead to an excessively pared-down style, if we are going to be left using only six items from the 'toolbox' as Stephen King calls it. And we don't often use exclamations, so that would leave us with only five.

Writers who I have always admired since a teenager are: Nathaniel West - Miss Lonelyhearts, The Day of the Locust and A Cool Million.

Georges Simenon – everything, there's 53 books of his in English and French so far on the shelves here.

And then I discovered Janet Frame. The Daylight and the Dust is a selection from four collections of her short stories. Her novel Angel at my Table is the best-known of her 20 works and was filmed by Jane Campion. Also from New Zealand, she is a modern Katherine Mansfield. Her writing is seamless, enticing and a joy to read.

52452434R10073

Made in the USA
Lexington, KY
20 September 2019